# YOUR SECRET SMILE

by Suzanne Ross Jones

## *Getting On With Life*

THE buzz hit with a force that left Grace Anderson reeling. The news was all over town – Sean McIver was back.

"You can't hide yourself away." Lizzie topped their coffees up with milk and handed one to Grace.

"I'm not hiding." Grace took her mug and gave a shrug.

"You've been stuck in your flat for the past week." There was a jingle of bangles as Lizzie threw the empty milk carton into the bin and moved to join Grace at the kitchen table. "You can't let him do this."

"I'm not letting him do anything, but seeing him is going to be weird. I don't want to bump into him before I'm ready."

"Seriously, Grace. Get it over with." Lizzie took a sip of her drink and cast a sympathetic glance towards her friend. "When you do, you'll see what an insignificant little pipsqueak he is and realise you've wasted the past eight years of your life pining over a guy who doesn't deserve you."

Grace flushed.

"I have not been pining."

Lizzie raised an eyebrow.

"OK, I was a little broken-hearted to begin with, but I got over it and got on with my life."

Lizzie gave a short nod.

"You did eventually pull yourself together – I'll give you that. But it took a while." Lizzie offered an apologetic smile in response to Grace's frown. "I'm sorry, but it's nothing your own mother wouldn't say if she was here."

Grace nodded. Her parents were away and she hadn't told them yet that Sean was back. She knew they'd advise her to keep her distance, but how could she do that when they would be working together?

"At least I don't have to worry about my parents' reactions for a while," she admitted weakly. They weren't due back from their six-month world cruise for a while yet.

"And as they're not around, it's up to me to make you face the truth. The fact you're hiding away makes it seem as though you might still have feelings for him."

"No," Grace denied. "I haven't thought about him in years." She sipped her coffee and refused to meet Lizzie's eyes.

It wasn't quite true that she hadn't thought about Sean. Sometimes, when she was feeling low, she did let herself wonder what might have been if he hadn't given in to his urge to travel. Or if she'd been able to go with him.

"Well, you'll have to face him before next week. You don't want your first meeting in years to be in the staff room."

Grace frowned.

"I can't believe he's a teacher." He'd left town because he wanted to travel. He hadn't wanted responsibilities or to be tied down. It was hard to imagine him settled in a respected role in the town he'd claimed was too quiet. "I can't believe, with all the schools in the world to choose from, he's taken a job at the one where I teach."

"And it's exactly because he's working at our school that

it's daft to let this get to you. You can't show any sign of weakness or the pupils will pounce."

"That's true." Grace knew Lizzie was talking good sense – teenagers could be very perceptive.

"So why not prove to the world you're not bothered? Besides, it's not only our pupils you have to worry about. Everyone in town's waiting to see how you react."

Grace felt her face flush.

"Really? They have nothing better to do?"

"You know as well as I do that they don't."

"I suppose." But while the quiet life in Montcraig had been one of the things that had driven Sean away, the peace and tranquillity were two of the reasons Grace loved living here so much. She sighed.

"Sometimes it's just too quiet here," Lizzie continued.

"There's nothing wrong with the quiet life."

"Pity you feel like that, because I'm having a party." Lizzie grinned. "Tomorrow night. A final fling before we all have to go back to school next week."

Immediately Grace was suspicious.

"You invented the party to tempt me out of the house." Lizzie smiled.

"Maybe, but it's a good idea. I can't imagine why I didn't think of it sooner." Lizzie drank the last of her coffee and took her mug over to the sink. "You will come, won't you?"

Grace smiled. Lizzie's parties were always fun. And even if the gathering was being engineered to get Grace out of the house, Lizzie's intentions were the best.

"Of course I will."

"Good. I'll see you at eight." There was more jangling of bangles as she gave Grace a quick hug. "Gotta go. People to call. Party plans to make."

Feeling a little brighter than she had all week, Grace smiled as her friend let herself out. Lizzie was a whirlwind – no other word for it. She arrived, she turned worlds upside-down and then she left, leaving upheaval in her wake.

But this was upheaval in a good way. It made Grace get things straight in her head. Hiding, Lizzie had accused her of. Grace hadn't rationalised it as such, but she hadn't been out of her flat for a week – not since she'd heard about her teenage sweetheart being back in town.

"This is ridiculous," she muttered. Grace had never been a coward. She'd always faced any difficulties head on. She realised now that people would be watching her carefully, waiting for a reaction whenever Sean's name was mentioned.

But she could deal with it.

She found her jacket and handbag. All too soon she'd be back in the classroom, trying to convince a group of unruly teenagers that algebra was the most fascinating subject in the universe. She was all kinds of daft to be wasting her last days of holiday moping around the house.

Besides, she had no bread and Lizzie had used the last of the milk in their coffees. She could murder a cup of tea and some hot, buttered toast.

She forced a smile and headed out to the local shop. She recognised her mistake when the shopkeeper perked up as soon as she noticed Grace had stepped over the threshold.

Trying to ignore the pair of eyes she could feel on her, she picked up a basket and scooted around the mini-supermarket. But there was no avoiding the inquisition when the time to pay came.

"Why do you think he came back after all this time?" Pam McGregor asked when Grace approached the counter with her basket of shopping.

"No idea." She didn't even pretend she didn't know who Pam was talking about. "But I'd like to pay for my shopping, if you don't mind."

Grace refused to offer the encouragement of making eye contact, but that didn't deter the shopkeeper. It was well known that, when there was the prospect of gossip, Pam was seldom put off.

"So, you haven't seen him yet?" she asked as she whizzed the items in Grace's basket through the till and rang up the total.

Grace smiled and forced her face to reveal nothing more than mild interest in the conversation. Sean was nothing to her now, and he hadn't been anything to her for a very long time. Her shock at the news of his return was normal. It didn't mean she had feelings for him. People needed to accept it and move on.

Knowing she was over him didn't stop her heart racing as she gathered her shopping and walked out on to the pavement. It didn't stop the thrill of anticipation when she spotted a tall, dark-haired man in the street, concentrating on the screen of his mobile phone. But, however much she told herself she didn't want to see Sean, she knew she was deluding herself when her heart plummeted as the man popped the mobile back into his pocket and turned.

"Hi, Ed." She was genuinely pleased to see the head of English, even if in her heart she couldn't quite forgive him for not being Sean.

"Hello, Grace. Enjoying the holidays?"

"I am, but it will be good to get back to work. The pupils drive me crazy at times with their cheek, but I do miss them."

"I know what you mean." Ed laughed. "Are you going to Lizzie's party tomorrow?"

Grace smiled.

"I don't believe it. She only just decided she was having a party. She didn't hang about with the invitations."

"She sent around a text. It only just arrived."

Grace nodded. That was exactly Lizzie's style – deciding on an impromptu party and the quickest means available to invite guests.

"Yes, I am going. What about you?"

Ed gave a half smile.

"Yes, I'll be there. Although it might be better for my peace of mind if I gave it a miss."

Grace offered a sympathetic smile and patted Ed's arm. It was such a shame – he was a lovely man and perfect for Lizzie, but Lizzie remained oblivious.

"I saw her over the holidays, you know. We worked together on a play for the drama group."

Grace nodded.

"She told me."

It was painful to see the hope in his eyes as he waited to hear what else Lizzie might have said about him. But the truth was that had been all, and she wasn't going to be the one to rub that fact in.

"Why don't you tell her how you feel?" she suggested.

"She's not interested."

"But how do you know? What do you have to lose by telling her?"

"At least I have her as a friend at the moment. If she guessed . . ." He gave an awkward shrug and Grace's heart went out to him. "Well, it might ruin even that."

If only Ed could pluck up the courage to tell her. Grace seemed to be wasting her time thinking about "if onlys" today, and they weren't any good for anyone.

"We could go to Lizzie's together," she suggested as they began to walk down the main street together. "Provide mutual moral support."

"Why do you need . . . ?" He broke off mid-sentence and frowned as realisation dawned. "Ah. Sorry, Grace. Yes, that's a good idea."

They walked in silence for a moment and stopped as they approached the old theatre. This was where they'd be parting company to head in opposite directions to their respective homes, but instead of saying goodbye, Ed nodded towards the *For Sale* sign on the old building.

"What do you think about this?"

She winced.

"I only hope it's not snapped up by some property developer and converted into flats."

"Or even worse, not bought at all and allowed to deteriorate further."

She looked up at the sorry old building and shuddered.

"That can't be allowed to happen."

Ed nodded.

"A few of us were talking about the possibility a day or two ago. We think there might be a solution – a way to preserve the building, and to keep it as a theatre."

"But it hasn't been a proper theatre for years. It's been a bingo hall for the past two decades."

"All right – a way to renovate and reinstate it as a theatre. I reckon we could do with a cultural centre in town again."

She stopped walking and glanced at the old theatre again.

"OK," she said. "I'm listening. What can we do?"

"If it was to be bought by local people, who loved the building and the town, it might solve all our problems." He put the suggestion out there and waited for Grace to react.

"But it would cost a fortune."

"Not necessarily. Property prices are depressed at the moment and this building needs a lot of work doing to it. It's mostly a cosmetic freshen and update, but I'm sure it will mean there's room to negotiate on the price."

"But still . . . Who in town could possibly afford it?"

Ed's steady gaze met hers.

"How about all of us?"

She shook her head. She couldn't see it.

"It would be a legal and practical nightmare. Everyone would want to impose their own ideas. War would break out."

He laughed.

"We've got two lawyers and an accountant already interested in keeping the peace. It will all be official – with a watertight contract to keep us straight and a committee to keep us all in line."

"Seems you've thought of everything."

He smiled and glanced up at the theatre again.

"We hope we have. This could make a real difference to the town. So, what do you think?"

She thought about his suggestion and realised how much sense it made.

"It would bring the community together."

"There's a meeting in the Montcraig Hotel next week to talk about it. I hope you can make it."

She nodded.

"I'll be there."

"Great. I'm going to photocopy some flyers, but if you could spread the word in the meantime that would be helpful. We're trying to get as many people as possible involved."

"Happy to."

"Thanks. I'll see you tomorrow." With a short wave he walked in the direction of his home.

Grace paused on the pavement for a moment after he'd gone and looked up at the old building again. Ed's plan could actually work. Excitement made her grin. This was such a good idea for the town. She couldn't believe nobody had thought of it before.

She was still smiling as she turned and slammed into a hard male chest. Startled, she looked up into a pair of bright blue eyes and her breath caught.

"Sean." Her voice was barely audible. Even though she'd expected to see him ever since she'd heard he was back, it was still a shock to find him here.

She felt a thud at her feet as her shopping bag fell from her fingers. Feeling suddenly faint, she staggered back a few steps, off the pavement and straight on to the road. The blast of a car's horn had her turning her startled face towards the oncoming vehicle into whose path she had stepped.

# *Old Friends*

SEAN watched in disbelief, his heart pounding frantically against his chest as the car got closer. It was going to hit Grace – no way could it possibly avoid her unless she moved off the road. And she didn't seem to be going anywhere.

He knew he should do something, but he was helpless as panic held him rooted to the spot.

It took a screech of tyres on tarmac to galvanise him into action. With a surge of adrenalin lending him breathtaking speed, he stepped forward and scooped her up. He was breathing hard as he stepped out of harm's way and the car screeched to a halt only inches away.

Relief made him gather her close and bury his face in her hair. He closed his eyes. She smelled of shampoo and the same light floral scent she'd worn as a teenager.

"Sean?" she questioned, her voice uncertain. "What are you doing?"

He lifted his head and his gaze met brown eyes wide with fright.

"Saving your life." His voice was harsher than it should have been and he hated himself for it, but he couldn't quite forget she could have been badly injured, or even killed.

A soft blush washed up over her pale cheeks.

"Well, you seem to have done a good job. Thank you."

Despite being cross she'd put herself in danger, he grinned. She'd always been able to cheer his mood with only a word or a glance – he'd forgotten that. He hadn't forgotten how pretty she was, though.

"Are you OK?"

"Yes, I'm fine. I think it's safe to put me down now."

He suddenly found he didn't want to let her go. She felt as though she belonged in his arms. Yet again he found himself wishing he hadn't left her all those years ago. It had taken him all of five minutes to realise he shouldn't have gone without her, but he'd been too young and too foolish to admit his mistake.

"Sean?" Her voice was uncertain. "Can you put me down, please?"

He nodded and, with great reluctance, set her down safely on the pavement beside him. Her brown eyes were large in her unnaturally pale face, and she brushed an unsteady hand through her shoulder-length blonde curls.

"Oh, Grace, are you OK?" The middle-aged woman who blustered towards them was red in the face, her panic visible.

Sean winced as he recognised his new boss, Harriet Roberts, the head of the school he was due to start work in next week.

Great, his new employer had witnessed him chasing another member of her staff into oncoming traffic. Not the best start.

Looking for a distraction, he picked up Grace's shopping bag from where she'd dropped it on the pavement.

Grace managed a faint smile

"I'm fine, thanks, Harriet." Although she felt anything but fine as she swayed alarmingly.

"What happened? You stepped right out in front of me. I don't know how I would have missed you if Sean hadn't stepped in."

"Sorry I gave you a fright." Grace glanced across at Sean and gave a sad half smile. "I didn't mean to step out on to the road."

Harriet glanced between the two of them and she frowned.

"You two working together isn't going to be a problem, I hope. I mean, you broke up so long ago."

"There's no problem," Grace rushed to assure their boss. "I was a little surprised to see Sean today, that's all. But it's always good to meet an old friend.

Harriet nodded, seemingly satisfied this potential for friction in the workplace would come to nothing.

"Good. Exactly as I thought. Well, if everyone's OK, I'd better get going."

They watched as the head teacher's car disappeared around the corner and then Sean turned to her. He was thoroughly deflated. She'd well and truly put him in his place.

"An old friend?"

There was a glimmer of something that might have been sadness – or regret – in her soft brown eyes. Did she wish she'd left with him as much as he still wished he'd waited for her? But even as he prepared to say something, the shadow in her gaze was gone and she smiled.

"Isn't that what we are?" She reclaimed her shopping bag from him and there was a defiant gleam in her eyes as she dared him to argue.

He shrugged.

"I suppose you're right." He glanced across the road to the café. "Do you have time for a coffee?"

She hesitated, then looked across the road and frowned.

"Or tea? I'll treat you," he added hopefully.

She shook her head.

"I don't know, Sean. It seems busy in there."

"My place then? I'm only two minutes away."

"I know that." She smiled. "Within two hours of you moving in everyone in town knew where you lived."

He laughed. The intrusion of town gossip might have been irritating, but he knew they all meant well. And he'd missed the caring way they all looked out for each other.

"I have biscuits," he coaxed. "Chocolate biscuits."

The corners of her mouth curved upwards.

"In that case, how can I refuse?"

It was the laugh that did it. She'd been so intent on keeping her distance, but when he'd laughed she'd been reminded of the old Sean. Her Sean.

She knew they could never be more than friends now – too much time had passed – but still a part of her cared. And it would be good to catch up.

Besides, she was still a bit wobbly on her feet from the shock of running into him as she had, not to mention her near miss with Harriet's car. A cup of tea and a biscuit would restore her to normality and she'd be able to deal with him as though he was just another friend.

He unlocked the door to his terraced cottage and she walked in, searching around for any clues about the man Sean had grown into. But his place gave very little away. It could be best described as functional and not in the least homely. No surprise, really, given how short a time he'd lived here.

"I'm still getting settled," he said and a shiver ran down her spine, because it seemed almost as though he'd read her thoughts.

That's what it had been like between them in the old days. They were on the same wavelength, he'd always said. But not any longer – she refused to allow it. The affinity they'd shared had been severed when he'd left. This had been a coincidence, nothing more. It couldn't be anything else.

"I suppose, being an art teacher, you'll want to put your own stamp on the place?"

He smiled.

"That's the idea."

He stood awkwardly in front of her and she got the feeling he was going to say something her intuition warned her she wasn't going to like. She didn't want apologies or explanations. She didn't want to go over the past. She wanted to move forward as she had been doing for the past eight years.

"I was promised tea." Her words came out in a rush, as though she thought speaking quickly would prevent him from telling her what was on his mind.

Sean hesitated for a moment and a glimmer of hope shone in his eyes.

"Grace, I thought maybe we could . . ."

"And biscuits," she added quickly. More than anything else, she didn't want him to suggest they rekindle their relationship, because there was no way she was taking chances with her heart again.

He nodded, a lock of hair falling across his forehead.

"OK, Grace. Come through to the kitchen and we'll find you those biscuits."

The kitchen was as stark and plain as the rest of the house – or at least the bits of the house she'd seen on her way through. She put her shopping down on the small table and took a seat.

"I can only stay five minutes." She got her excuse in before he tried to persuade her otherwise. "I've got to get the milk back before it turns sour."

He nodded.

"I'd better get the kettle on, then."

She tucked into the biscuits while he made the tea.

"Sugar's good for shock," she told him in reply to his raised eyebrow when she picked up her third.

"You didn't seem that traumatised at the time." He brought the tea over and set it on the table.

No, she hadn't been traumatised. Not about her near miss with the car, in any case. But even while she knew she'd probably have nightmares tonight about Harriet running her over, she had been too preoccupied with Sean to worry about it at the time.

"Delayed reaction."

She'd forgotten his eyes were quite so blue and that his smile could set her heart fluttering. But her reaction to him was only an echo of feelings from long ago. She'd told Harriet they were nothing more than friends, and she was sure it was the truth. Or at least it would be. She needed to put in a little work on being unaffected, that was all.

She drank her tea as quickly as she could, even though it was still far too hot for her liking. She knew accepting his offer of tea had been the right thing, but she didn't want to prolong the meeting. There was no doubt seeing him again had shaken her. She needed to be on her own now, to build up her armour again.

"Thank you for the tea and the biscuits." She got up and grabbed her shopping bag.

He got to his feet, but thankfully didn't try to persuade her to stay.

"Perhaps we'll bump into each other again before school starts back."

She nodded.

"Perhaps."

If they did meet again, she knew now she would be strong enough to cope. Sean McIver was an old boyfriend and a new colleague, nothing more. The fact she was able to walk out of here with her nerves intact confirmed those facts.

As soon as she got home she picked up the phone and called Lizzie.

"Hi, it's Grace."

"What did you forget to tell me earlier?"

Grace laughed and slipped on to the nearest chair.

"Nothing, but I did see Ed when I popped to the shop." She paused, hoping for a reaction that might give her hope her friend had realised how perfect a couple she and Ed would make. She was disappointed when it didn't happen.

"He's accepted the invitation for tomorrow so we're up to a dozen people now."

Lizzie was so perceptive when it came to other people, but she couldn't seem to see her co-worker was crazy about her.

"He was talking about the old theatre. Has he mentioned it to you?"

"He said something. Seemed to think it would be good for the drama group."

Grace settled back into her chair.

"A number of people are thinking of getting together to put in an offer for it," she explained. "There's a meeting next week. We should go."

Lizzie groaned.

"But we're back at school next week. It's going to be such a busy time."

"It's for the good of the community," Grace coaxed, smiling as she imagined her friend's dismayed expression at the thought of another item to add to her workload.

"Maybe I could spare an hour to go and find out what it's all about." There was a brief silence and then Lizzie sighed. "I'd better be going. I've a lot to do before tomorrow night. That's unless you have any news?"

"Actually, I do have something to tell you." She paused for a moment, knowing once she shared the news, Lizzie would want to talk some more. "I took your advice. I faced Sean McIver."

There was a shriek from the other end.

"Good for you. Tell me everything."

Grace missed out the bit about stepping in front of Harriet's car – there were some foolish reactions a girl didn't want to share even with her best friend. But she told Lizzie about the tea.

"I ate three biscuits without blinking," she confessed.

"Never mind the biscuits. Did he say where he's been? What he's been up to all these years? Where his family are now? If they'd stayed around he would have had reason to pop by sooner."

"No. No. And no," Grace replied. "To be honest I didn't ask."

"Oh, Grace." Lizzie sighed loudly. "You're hopeless. Well, I suppose I'll have to interrogate him myself. How would you feel if I asked him to the party?"

Grace shrugged, even though there was nobody there to see her.

"It's your party. It's up to you who you invite."

"I won't if you'd rather I didn't. But I'm rather hoping you're immune to his charms after all these years."

"My inoculations are up to date where Sean McIver is concerned. And the booster from this afternoon has taken effect."

"Good. I don't think it would be good for you to go down that route again."

"Couldn't agree more." Grace sighed down the phone. Lizzie was so right – Sean was no good for her. A man who could leave her broken-hearted and not even send a postcard in all those years wasn't worthy of her interest.

"Inviting him would be the right thing to do. I've asked all the other teachers, though thankfully a number are away on holiday. I don't know what I'd have done if they'd all agreed to come. My house isn't big enough." She paused for a moment. "But it's up to you. If you'd rather I didn't ask, I won't."

"Go ahead," she said without hesitation.

She had to get used to seeing him around the place, after all. And now she'd managed to survive that awkward first meeting, seeing Sean McIver in a social setting had to be the next test.

"OK, if you're sure you don't mind, I'll ask him."

# Party Time

THE building was practically dancing along to the thumping of the bass. Lights shone from every window and the unmistakeable sounds of people having fun reached out to where Sean stood on the pavement.

It was obvious Lizzie still knew how to throw a party.

He breathed in the cool evening air and glanced up at the house. He'd travelled the world on his own, made friends with strangers. And yet he was reluctant to join this gathering, even though he'd known a number of the guests from a childhood spent in Montcraig.

He took another deep breath. This was daft. It had been his decision to come back. He was in control. But however much his head told him to go in, his legs refused to move.

Grace had made it pretty obvious earlier she wanted as little to do with him as possible. And, even though he'd ended their relationship by leaving, it still hurt him.

A couple walked past him into the house and, without warning, he was transported back to the last time he'd accepted one of Lizzie's invitations. That time the party had been at her parents' house and she'd thrown it to celebrate the end of their school days. He'd gone with Grace. That had been the night he'd asked her to confirm their plans to go travelling – and the night they'd broken up.

He shook his head to clear the memories away and stepped towards the house. Standing out here was achieving nothing. He had colleagues to mingle with.

A random partygoer let him in and he saw Grace at once. Even with the crowds enjoying themselves, his gaze homed in on her with precision. She hadn't noticed him. She was deep in conversation with a man he didn't recognise and he was reluctant to interrupt.

"Sean, you made it." Lizzie arrived at his side with a smile on her face, her voice raised so she could be heard about the noise. "I was starting to think you wouldn't come."

He smiled back. He'd always liked Lizzie, even though she'd given him a piece of her mind when his plans to leave without Grace became known. But she'd only been showing concern for Grace, so how could he dislike her for that?

"Wouldn't have missed it for the world," he replied, opting not to mention he'd very nearly gone home rather than knock on the door.

"Let's introduce you to some people." She pulled him by the arm and took him over to Grace and her mystery man.

"You know Grace, of course." Lizzie cast a concerned glance over at her friend, but when Grace smiled she visibly relaxed. "And this is Ed Price, head of English and Drama."

Ed's handshake was firm and his expression friendly. Either he didn't know about Sean and Grace's shared history, or else he wasn't interested in Grace in a romantic sense.

Even though he had no right, Sean rather hoped it was the latter.

Grace had been aware of Sean from the moment he came into the room, but she'd kept her gaze averted on purpose. She fully intended to be friendly, but that was all. Even if an echo of the old feelings still lingered, she couldn't risk a repetition of what had happened when they'd been teenagers. No way was she going to allow the same man to break her heart twice. No matter how blue his eyes or how wicked his grin.

"Lizzie, do you fancy a dance?" Ed made the request sound casual and Grace, knowing how much courage it had taken for him to ask, held her breath, hoping her friend would agree. Even though it would leave her on her own in this corner with Sean, which was the last thing she wanted.

Lizzie ran her hand through her long red hair, bracelets jangling at her wrist.

"Why not?"

They moved into the centre of the room and joined the other dancing couples, leaving Grace alone with Sean. Or as alone as it was possible to be at one of Lizzie's parties.

He leaned forward to speak and the warm tones of his aftershave tickled her nose.

"You look very nice. The dress suits you."

His clumsy compliment suggested he was as awkward with the situation as she was. She offered a half-hearted smile. She knew she had to say something or their working relationship would be unbearable. She loved her job and she didn't want any tensions or unresolved personal issues to spoil that.

Whatever he was back for, whether he was interested in rekindling their romantic relationship or not, she had to set boundaries. For her own sake. As part of those boundaries he had to know it wasn't OK to comment on her appearance, however innocuous the comment seemed.

"You don't have to do this, Sean."

She saw confusion in his blue eyes.

"What am I doing?"

"Making polite talk. We both know the situation. We once meant something to each other, but it was a long time ago." She felt her face flush with embarrassment. She might be getting this spectacularly wrong. Maybe he was only being friendly. But she couldn't take the risk he might still harbour hope in her direction. "You don't have to tell me if you think I look nice these days. In fact, you really shouldn't notice that kind of thing at all."

He nodded and his too-long hair fell across his forehead. She itched to reach out and brush it back, but thankfully controlled the urge. It would not have been appropriate. Particularly as she was in the middle of telling him there was no prospect of anything of a romantic nature ever happening between them.

"So what are we to each other now?"

She shrugged.

"Colleagues. Acquaintances."

"Old friends," he supplied, repeating the words she'd told Harriet yesterday.

"Yes." She smiled, relieved to be reminded of this very convenient label for whatever might be left between them. "Old friends. And there's no need to be awkward and make small talk with old friends. And there's definitely no need to notice if an old friend looks nice."

He nodded and leaned back against the wall.

"So, is it OK if an old friend asks after your parents?"

She nodded. Parents were a safer topic.

"They're fine. They're away on a cruise at the moment. Dad's taken early retirement and Mum . . ." She paused, knowing how lucky they were her mother was in a position to go on any kind of holiday. "Mum's not been too well."

"Sorry to hear that. Is she OK now?"

Grace nodded.

"We hope so." She couldn't meet his eye. She didn't want him to notice the accusatory gleam she suspected he'd find there. That was definitely not something an old friend should see.

When he'd left town, her mother had already been diagnosed. That had been the real reason she hadn't gone with him when he'd asked. She didn't want to be on the other side of the world while her mother was receiving treatment.

Even now a part of her blamed him for going. She'd needed him and he should have known that.

"How about your parents?" she asked him. "How are they?"

"Both fine." He grinned. "They love the city. The plan had always been to move back once we'd all left home, and they haven't regretted it once."

Sean was the youngest of four brothers. His parents had moved to Montcraig because they had wanted their children to grow up in the country, but Mary and Steven McIver had never really settled in the small town. A part of them had stayed in the city where they'd lived all their lives before they'd moved here. It hadn't been a surprise to anyone when they'd moved away shortly after Sean left on his travels.

She smiled as Harriet passed by, looking very glamorous in high heels and carrying a tray of glasses towards the kitchen. As she watched, Harriet tripped. Grace didn't know quite how it happened. For countless seconds, the head teacher flew through the air with an expression of horror on her face. The music stopped and everyone held their breath as she landed with an almighty crash on top of the tray, which was now shattered glass.

Pandemonium broke out. There was talking. Someone screamed as they caught sight of the injured Harriet. Then everyone surged forward at once, all trying to help.

"Please, keep back." Sean used his large frame to keep the crowds away from Harriet as Grace stepped forward to ascertain the extent of the damage. "Give her some room."

Grace would have been impressed by the way he controlled the situation, but she was too busy seeing if Harriet was all right. Thankfully, apart from a nasty cut on her hand, not much harm seemed to have been done.

"So silly," she muttered, trying to get up.

"Keep still," Grace warned. "There's a lot of broken glass around. Now, apart from your hand, are you hurt?"

"No, I'm fine." Harriet tried to get up again, but this time – satisfied there were no bones broken – Grace and Sean helped.

"What happened?" Lizzie asked as she came in from the kitchen, her face pale.

"I tripped over my own feet. It must be the shoes – they're new. I knew I shouldn't have worn them tonight."

Grace glanced down.

"Well, they are lovely shoes. I can see why you'd want to show them off."

"They'll be going to the charity shop first thing in the morning." Harriet, flustered, glanced around at the interested crowd. "I'm fine, everyone, thank you. Get back to your dancing while I clear up this mess."

"You're not clearing anything up," Lizzie told her sternly. "I'll do that in a minute. Your hand needs to be seen by a doctor. You might need stitches."

"I'm fine," she protested. "Really."

But someone brought a clean tea towel just the same and Lizzie wrapped it carefully and loosely around Harriet's hand.

"I'll drive you to the hospital," Sean offered.

It seemed as though Harriet was going to refuse, so Grace jumped in.

"That's a good idea, Sean. Harriet, Lizzie's right, you must get that hand looked at."

"Here's your coat," Lizzie added, draping the garment over her shoulders.

Before she could object further, Harriet was sitting in the passenger seat of Sean's car and everyone was waving them off.

"You seemed awfully keen to get out of there," Harriet commented when they were driving towards the hospital.

Sean indicated to turn right at the end of the street.

"My motive is irrelevant. You need to be seen by a medical professional."

Harriet sighed.

"OK. Well, I'm sorry you had to leave on my account."

He laughed.

"My excuse might be valid, but you're right, I wasn't heartbroken to get out of there."

"You didn't take your eyes off her all night."

He grimaced. Harriet liked to get straight to the point. That much was obvious. But he was in no mood to discuss Grace.

"I was hardly there five minutes. And I was speaking to her for two of those five."

Harriet sighed.

"OK, you stared at her the whole five minutes you were in there – even when you weren't speaking to her."

"Nothing wrong with looking at a pretty girl." He tried to make light of the observation, but he knew his voice sounded flat.

"I run a happy ship," she told him. "I don't want any friction or upsets at my school."

"There won't be any. The last thing I'd ever want to do would be to upset Grace."

"You upset her plenty when you left Montcraig before."

He nodded.

"I know. I regret it very much."

"I need to know, Sean, what's going on exactly?"

Even though his eyes were on the road, he could feel Harriet's keen gaze boring into him and he felt there was nowhere to hide.

"Nothing. We're old friends, like she told you yesterday."

"Old friends, my eye. You're still in love with her," Harriet accused.

How could Sean deny it when it was the truth?

"You can't hurt her again," she warned. "I know what happened was long ago and you were both young, but you didn't see how upset she was after you went away. If you have any feelings at all left for her, you'll leave her alone."

He brought the car to a halt in the hospital car park and turned in his seat to look at his boss.

"And what if I can't leave her alone?"

Harriet shook her head.

"You must."

## *Leaving Grace Alone*

S EAN thought a lot about Harriet's words over the next few days. She was right, of course, he knew she was. He had no business messing with Grace's life again.

But that didn't mean he didn't want to.

He'd thought about her a lot while he'd been away. And, even though he'd only seen her a couple of time since he got back – and both those meetings had been brief – he knew he wanted to see more of her. Although she had made it pretty clear she wasn't interested in anything other than the most casual of friendships.

He should have taken the hint when she'd stepped out into the road to get away from him. If a woman was prepared to face oncoming traffic rather than talk to him it had to be a bad sign.

He put the paintbrush down and surveyed his handiwork. The living-room was now a dramatic red, cosy and warm and all ready for the autumn that was only just around the corner. He couldn't help wondering what Grace might make of it.

She'd noticed the house's bland appearance – how could she not have? – and this room was the last to be transformed. He hoped she'd like it. And he hoped he'd have cause to invite her around again soon so he could find out if she did.

Keeping busy had meant he'd been out of the path of temptation: If he didn't see Grace, he wouldn't be able to make a fool of himself by chasing after her.

He was tidying away when the doorbell sounded. Startled, he looked up. Nobody had bothered him all weekend, so it was a shock to have a visitor.

"Ed," he greeted when he opened the door. "Come in."

He saw the other man's nose twitch as he stepped into the hallway.

"Been decorating?"

"Just putting my own stamp on the place." He smiled as he realised he'd used the same words Grace had last week. "I've got some paintings to put up on the walls, but I'm pretty much done now."

Ed nodded, but didn't offer an opinion.

"I was wondering if you'd heard there's a town meeting tonight."

"About the old theatre? Yes, someone put a flyer through my door."

"I do hope we'll see you there. We're trying to get as much support as possible together."

Sean rubbed his chin.

"I really hadn't thought about it."

"Most of the teachers are going to be there," he said. "It would be good to provide a united front. After all, the school will benefit."

"In what way?" Sean asked.

"We'd be able to use it for concerts and plays, for a start. And a few of us are involved in a co-curricular drama group – it would be good to have somewhere proper to meet and put on our productions. You could even put on art exhibitions of the pupils' work there."

"What about the assembly hall?"

Ed frowned.

"In an ideal world, yes, we would be able to use it for all those things. But in reality it's barely big enough for all the pupils, let alone for their parents and grandparents as well."

Sean could see the sense in the plans for the town to take over the old theatre.

"It would be good for the community, too," he said thoughtfully. "Everyone would have to work together to bring it off."

"Exactly. So, what do you say? Are you interested in coming along tomorrow night? Unless, of course, you're not planning on staying in Montcraig in the long term."

"I'm staying," he said. "I've travelled the world and realised this is the only place that feels like home." He missed out the part where he was sure it only felt like home because this was where Grace lived. "How about I put the kettle on and you can tell me a bit more about your plans for this theatre."

\*　　　　　\*　　　　　\*　　　　　\*

"So, are you all set for tomorrow?" Grace asked Lizzie, who was busy sorting through a pile of books at her kitchen table.

"Just about." She smiled. "Clothes all laid out, shoes polished. What more is there to do?"

"Get through tonight?" Grace suggested. She knew Lizzie wasn't keen on this town meeting, but Grace was determined to persuade her.

"Aw, Grace, I don't know. I was kind of thinking a nice bath and an early night – some relaxation in preparation for the rest of the week."

"Anyone would think you didn't like school." Grace laughed because it was a ridiculous suggestion. There wasn't a single teacher at school more dedicated than Lizzie.

"You know I love my job." She smiled. "But I also love my holidays."

"The theatre would be good for the drama group." Grace played her winning hand.

"I know, honey." Lizzie sighed loudly. "And I suppose that's why I can't say no."

The drama group was Lizzie's baby. She'd set it up from scratch with Ed two years ago. Most of the teenagers in town were involved and it had been very successful in cutting the rates of petty crime and teen loitering in the evenings.

"And, of course, Ed will be there." She glanced at Lizzie, hoping for a glimmer of a reaction. Nothing. This was hopeless. She was so tempted to blurt out the truth, but she knew Ed wouldn't thank her for it. And perhaps Lizzie wouldn't, either.

"Never mind Ed. What about Sean? Will he be there?"

Grace felt the blush on her cheek and cursed the fair skin that would make it obvious. She shouldn't be blushing at the mention of his name. She was a sophisticated, independent career woman, and sophisticated women didn't turn bright red at the mention of the teenage sweethearts they had lost so many years ago. Particularly when they were trying to convince everyone, including themselves, that they had no interest in that particular lost sweetheart.

"How on earth would I know?"

Lizzie winced in reaction to Grace's harsh tone and left her books, coming over to Grace's side and giving her a quick hug.

"Sorry." She grimaced as she went back to her task. "I didn't mean to upset you. It was only my clumsy way of asking if you'd seen him in the past few days."

Grace shook her head.

"The last I saw of him was when he left yours to take Harriet to hospital."

For some reason, not seeing him had upset her, which was odd when she was still pretty sure she didn't actually want to see him. She supposed it was more the fact that he hadn't tried to see her. She would have expected him to make a bit of an effort.

It was irrational and illogical, but that was the kind of way she'd always been around Sean. Her emotions had always overruled her head. And now his return had thrown her off balance; made her wary and careful. And yet, still her heart beat a little faster at the thought she might see him.

"As far as I know, nobody's seen much of him since then." Lizzie tipped a pile of books into a large bag ready for school. "I was speaking to Pam McGregor in the shop this morning. She said he was in to buy groceries a few days ago, but other than that he's been locked away in his house."

"We shouldn't take any notice of Pam McGregor," Grace cautioned. "Her information isn't always the most reliable."

"I think this time's she's spot on. Nobody I know has seen him for days."

Grace wasn't about to admit it out loud, but she wondered why that was. He'd never been one to hide away, so what had changed? She wished she'd realised he'd been living the life of a recluse since his return, then she wouldn't have been on edge every time she'd left her own home. She'd thought, once she'd got that awkward meeting over and done with, things would be easier, but if anything they were more difficult.

She needed to build up a shield against him and she needed to do it fast.

"He's probably been decorating," she said at last. "He said he was planning to make his place more homely."

Lizzie frowned.

"He's the last person I'd expect to have a nesting instinct. Maybe he's changed."

Maybe he had. But Grace doubted it. A fun-loving boy who yearned to travel and who chased bright lights was hardly going to grow into a man who craved stability and wanted to live a quiet life in a place like Montcraig.

\*     \*     \*     \*

Sean had forgotten so many people lived in the small town, but when you saw them all squeezed into the function room at the Montcraig Hotel, it was impossible to ignore. Everyone, it seemed, was keen on the town buy-out of the old theatre and they all wanted in on the action.

The noise was deafening as everyone chatted and he stood at the back looking out for Grace. He could see her over the heads of the other people, to the back of the room. She was unmistakeable, her halo of blonde curls marking her out of the crowd. And that red hair next to her had to belong to Lizzie.

No point trying to get closer – he wouldn't stand a chance. There was barely room to breathe. He leaned back against the wall and folded his arms across his chest. Ed had been right – they did need a venue where the community could meet. The old theatre would be big enough for the entire town, with seats for everyone.

"Sean McIver, fancy that."

He forced his eyes away from Grace's hair and focused on the small woman standing next to him.

"Hello, Pam. How are you?"

Pam's beady stare fixed him to the spot.

"I'm fine. I can see you have your eye on a certain maths teacher."

He laughed. Pam McGregor was barely five feet tall, there was no way she'd be able to see who he'd been looking at.

"Was that an educated guess?"

She smiled.

"Who else would you be looking at with such an expression on your face?"

He shook his head. She meant well, but he didn't reply. It was bad enough that she suspected he was pining for Grace, but, at the moment, everything she thought she knew was supposition. It would be lethal to give her any concrete information. If he did it would be all around the village before he could say unrequited love.

That was exactly what he was suffering from, he realised now with blinding clarity. He still loved Grace – and she no longer loved him. Not that he blamed her. He hadn't been able to wait to leave town after they'd left school. When she'd told him she couldn't leave he should have re-evaluated his plans. Waited until she was ready to go with him.

Thankfully, the meeting began, diverting Pam's and his attention towards the front of the room. Ed called order and introduced the others who were standing at the front with him, even though most knew who they were already: Carol Parker, an architect, Steve Baker and Edward Charles who were both solicitors, and Evelyn Carter, accountant.

"We're very lucky to have this team of people prepared to donate their time to keep us right on this community project."

There was a smattering of applause and a murmuring of approval. Sean was impressed. It seemed the town meant business and with a team of professionals leading proceedings, it seemed they did have a hope of getting the project off the ground.

They talked costs; how many people they'd need to invest to make it manageable.

"We all have to be involved in some capacity," Ed told them. "We need as many members of the community as possible to invest actual funds. But we'll also be looking for folk to invest time. We want you all to be involved so that the whole town has an interest in the project."

There was more applause, louder this time.

"Once we've secured ownership of the property, we'll all have to work together and do what we can to make the building into the theatre we deserve."

There was a rousing cheer and more applause. Ed quickly gave an overview of likely costs and a list of work they thought would have to be done.

"Steve and Edward are ready to take names. If you're interested – and I hope most of you will be – come forward and add your names to the list before you go. You're not going to be committing yourselves to anything at this stage, just registering your interest. Then we can follow up with more information before you make a decision."

There was a rush of people towards the front of the room. Sean stood back and let them all get their names down. It wasn't as though he was in any hurry.

By the time his turn came to register his interest in the project, Grace was gone, which was probably just as well.

He wasn't supposed to be messing with Grace's life, he'd decided. And he'd decided what he wanted didn't matter. Harriet had been right – he had no right to go anywhere near her, so it was just as well she'd left before he got the chance to speak to her.

But as he stepped out on to the street he saw her up ahead. She drew him like a magnet, regardless of any sensible decision he'd made. Forgetting everything about keeping away from her being for the best, he caught up and fell into step beside her.

"Hello, Grace."

She missed a step and he reached out to grab her arm in an attempt to stop her stumbling.

"Hi," she said, quickly recovering her composure and stepping neatly out of his reach.

"Good turnout at the meeting."

"It was. Ed will be pleased. He's worked really hard on this project."

Sean tried not to grimace as Grace mentioned Ed again.

"You seem very fond of Ed."

A soft smile played about her lips.

"I am. He's a good friend."

Sean wanted to ask more about her definition of a good friend, and he wanted to know how Ed felt about Grace, but he knew he didn't have the right to ask those questions. However much he might want it to be, Grace's romantic life was none of his business.

They walked along in silence for a short time before Sean felt the need to say something.

"How was Lizzie's party after I left?"

"Quiet. Nobody felt like having fun when Harriet had been hurt. We tidied up and everyone drifted off home."

"That's a shame. It seemed to be going so well."

"It was, but it's hard to have fun when you're worried about someone."

"She's OK."

Grace nodded.

"I've spoken to her a couple of times so I know she'll be fine once the stitches are out. But at the time the accident took the shine off the evening."

He could understand that. Harriet had been quite shaken by the experience, it was only natural her staff would be concerned.

Without looking, Grace could see Sean on the periphery of her vision. He was tall and strong, his face more handsome than it had any right to be. But she refused to look at him openly as he walked beside her, and she didn't want to examine too closely why that might be.

"Are you nervous about tomorrow?" She was determined to keep the conversation neutral.

As they approached the old theatre, they both slowed their paces. It was only natural that, with the meeting still fresh in their minds, they took their time to consider the old building.

"Not really," he said with conviction. "Why would I be nervous?"

Her eyes narrowed as she gave into temptation to glance across. Once she had, it was hard to look away.

She gulped in a lungful of night air.

"Most people get nervous before starting a new job." She forced her gaze away from him and back on to the theatre. Looking at Sean McIver was dangerous, and there was no way she was falling into the trap again.

"This is hardly new to me. I've been a teacher before."

"But at a different school," she pointed out. Even to her own ears it sounded as though she wanted to talk him into being nervous. Which was nonsense – she was only talking about work to keep from veering into more personal territory.

"I was a pupil at Montcraig High during my own school days. Besides, I know a number of the teachers already."

They quickened their pace again and, when they approached the road where Sean's house was, he ignored the turning and kept walking towards Grace's house.

"Where are you going?" she asked.

"Seeing you home."

She blustered for a moment before replying.

"There's no need, Sean. I've managed to walk home on my own perfectly well without you for the past eight years."

Grace stopped mid-stride. Shocked at her own short tone, her eyes snapped up to his face. His eyes widened in surprise and then he smiled slowly and intimately, his gaze never leaving hers.

She felt a fluttering in the region of her heart and for a moment she couldn't breathe. With huge effort she gulped in a lungful of air and her gaze dropped to her feet.

"I'm sorry," she said. "I shouldn't have snapped at you."

"Come on, Grace," he said, his tone so soft it made her want to cry. "Let's get you home. We both have a busy day tomorrow."

## *Term Begins*

THERE was always a shock realisation of how quickly the school holidays had flown by when Grace had to prepare for the first day of term. It had been the same during her own school days and she'd never quite grown out of the sense of unreality that plagued her during the break. The unreality that made every day blend into the next and keeping track of time became impossible.

But school was her life and it was good to be going back.

Not so good to be standing in the pouring rain, staring hopelessly under the bonnet of her car and wondering if she might not be better catching the bus.

She vaguely heard another car slow to a stop beside her, its engine still running. Mildly curious, she turned to find Sean leaning out of the driver's window.

"Everything OK?"

No, it wasn't. But she didn't want him to know that.

"It won't start." She could have bitten off her tongue, but she knew there was little point in pretending everything was fine when it obviously wasn't. Even if he'd guessed she wasn't standing in a downpour for fun, it would have been a dead giveaway when she turned up an hour late to work.

"Do you know what's wrong?"

"I think the battery might be flat. I didn't use it much over the summer." There had been no need, as everything in Montcraig was within walking distance. Well, everything apart from Montcraig Academy, which stood up on the hill overlooking town a good two miles away. It was walkable on a good day, when she'd allowed enough time and was wearing sensible shoes, but definitely not easily negotiable in bad weather or in the very frivolous sandals she'd mistaken for a good idea for her first day back. Besides, she could feel her hair starting to frizz up already in the damp air, even though it was tucked safely inside the hood of her waterproof anorak. A walk through this rain would finish the job.

"Do you have jump leads?"

She shook her head.

"OK, hop in. I'll give you a lift to school and see if I can get your car going when we get back this afternoon."

"Sean, I . . ."

"Grace, please don't argue. There's no time. I'm not going to leave you here like this, but I really don't want to be late to work on my first day."

She hesitated for a second before locking her own car and slipping, dripping rainwater, into the passenger seat of his.

"Thank you for stopping. It was kind of you."

He sighed softly.

"I was hardly going to drive by and leave you in the rain." He took a quick glance down to her feet and she felt herself blush as he looked at her bare toes with their nails painted a shocking pink. "And we couldn't have such lovely feet getting wet now, could we?"

She frowned.

"They're already wet. The forecast was for sun."

He laughed softly and she felt her own mouth curve into an answering smile.

"That's better," he said.

And, despite the torrential rain, Grace's bad mood lifted as though the sun had peeked out from behind the clouds.

Sean parked as close to the main building as he could. He knew a little bit of water never hurt anyone, but he didn't like the thought of Grace's feet being cold and wet.

"This way," she told him as she dodged between puddles.

The place was eerily quiet as it generally was in any school on the first day the staff returned. The pupils weren't expected in until tomorrow. This was the chance for the teachers to get settled in, to make final preparations for lessons and to catch up with each other after the break.

Sean had hoped not to draw attention to himself when he arrived, but was given little choice given he was with Grace and they were there with minutes to spare. It seemed everyone was already in as they entered the staff room and endless pairs of eyes turned their way.

He smiled, but he could feel Grace squirm at his side.

"My car wouldn't start," she rushed to explain on the crest of a blush. "Sean offered me a lift."

They crossed the floor with all eyes still on them, then slipped into a couple of empty chairs near Lizzie.

"You OK, honey?" he heard Lizzie whisper.

Grace's blonde curls bounced as she nodded and she turned her attention to where Harriet stood, bandage on her hand, waiting for everyone to quieten down.

"This morning we have a motivational speaker coming in to discuss the benefits of positive thinking in the classroom," she told them.

A general groan went around the room.

"As if we don't have enough to do without listening to some new-age nonsense," someone muttered from the corner.

"Now, everyone," Harriet looked around. "Keep an open mind. You might learn something worthwhile."

"I doubt it," the same voice called back. Good-natured laughing swept through the room.

Sean immediately felt at home. This was like every other staff room he'd been in.

He caught up with Grace at lunchtime. She was in her classroom, a mountain of papers scattered over her desk.

"Hungry?" he asked from the door.

She looked up and, just for a moment, there was a glimmer of something in her eyes. Something that reminded him of the way she'd looked at him before he'd left Montcraig all those years ago. But before he could react it was gone and she glanced at her watch.

"Lunchtime already? I hadn't realised."

He stepped inside the classroom and pulled a chair towards her desk.

"I nipped into town and got these." He pulled sandwiches, soft drinks and cake from the shopping bag he was holding and sat down without being asked. "Enough for two."

He hid his uncertainty behind a veneer of normality and confidence as he pulled the packets open.

"What would you prefer? Cheese and tomato or tuna?" He held his breath and waited for her to tell him to get lost, but she didn't.

"We could share half of each?" She suggested, and that sounded pretty good to him.

Grace hadn't planned on a picnic lunch with an old boyfriend in her classroom, but it was turning out rather well. The fact he'd brought food to her meant she wouldn't have to abandon her work and go in search of lunch herself. Besides, she found she didn't quite have the heart to tell him to go away after he'd been so kind this morning.

She went over to a corner of the room and pulled a kettle and some cups from a cupboard.

"I'll make us some tea," she told him as she headed for the door in search of water. "Chilled soft drinks are nice, but a chilly damp day like today calls for something hot."

"Very true." He smiled and she couldn't help smiling back. It was nice to share a lighter moment with him after all the stress of his return to Montcraig.

The tea was made in a jiffy.

"I got some jump leads, too, while I was out," he told her as he took the cup she offered. "I'll drop you home after work and we can get your car started."

"There's no need. It might have stopped raining by then and I can walk and call the breakdown service." She glanced in hope towards the windows where angry clouds still loomed. It didn't look like that walk was going to happen today. "Or I can ask Lizzie for a lift," she finished weakly.

"Or you could make life easier for yourself and accept the help I'm offering. I'm not your enemy, Grace."

No, he'd never been her enemy, she knew that. But she had to put measures in place to protect her heart. When he was being this helpful, when he was sitting across the desk from her as gorgeous as he'd ever been, it was hard to remember to keep him at a distance.

"Second evening in a row you'll have seen me home," she said, half to herself. "I'm beginning to wonder how I ever managed to go anywhere on my own."

"Accepting help when you need it doesn't make you incapable. It just makes you sensible."

She sighed softly.

"I'm surprised you had time to go waltzing off to town to buy jump leads and sandwiches. Don't you have lessons to prepare for?"

She wasn't really surprised – it was no more than she would have expected of him. He was a free spirit and always would be. He'd take his classes a day at a time, making a mockery of her carefully constructed lesson plans.

"I did most of my preparation over the summer."

"Oh." OK, he had surprised her. "It's not like you to think that far ahead."

He smiled and picked up a sandwich.

"I'm not the same person I was."

"I gathered that."

"I know it must have seemed frivolous, but I was young back then and travelling was something I had to get out of my system."

"What changed your mind? Why did you come back?"

Sean studied his sandwich as though it was the most interesting thing on earth, then, slowly and deliberately, he bit into it. He wasn't going to answer. Instead, he chewed carefully and she held her breath.

Then he looked into her eyes, his own darkening to almost navy blue and she held her breath. She wished she hadn't asked. She'd made it more than clear she wasn't interested in anything other than friendship and, for the time being, he'd decided to play along with that. But her question could ruin all that.

"Maybe I missed the place," he said at last.

\*     \*     \*     \*

Grace's car started first time the next morning. Sean had sorted it last night, then she'd gone for a drive to recharge the battery. She made a mental note not to leave it sitting for almost an entire school holiday in future.

School, of course, was an entirely different prospect than it had been yesterday. Even though she arrived early, there were crowds of young people milling around, all eager to share their news and holiday stories with friends who lived out of town.

"Hey, miss!" A boy called from across the way as she got out of the car. "Did you enjoy your holidays?"

"I did, thank you, Callum." She smiled and made her way inside. Normally she would head to the staff room for a quick coffee, but she wanted to get settled before her registration class arrived.

If yesterday had been a surreal start after the holidays, today was vibrant and very real. She loved seeing the pupils at the start of term. She found their excitement infectious and she loved the potential each child had, if they worked hard, to excel.

She was still fizzing with the newness of it all when her fourth years started to come in and take their seats. Some offering a bright "Hello, miss", others mumbling incoherently, and one girl scuttling in, trying not to be seen.

Grace was concerned to see that Katie hadn't overcome her painful shyness over the holidays. Last year a number of teachers had raised concerns. It had generally been accepted she would settle in and become more sociable, but the way she was avoiding eye contact and sitting on her own in a corner, Grace guessed the problem had become worse.

She was about to call the class to attention when Sean popped his head around the door.

"Everything OK with the car this morning?"

What was he doing? His behaviour would make these young teenagers immediately curious, and they were as prone to gossip as their parents. Flustered, she looked up at him. He was looking neater than she'd ever seen him before – not in a suit, but this was Sean McIver, after all. He was wearing smart trousers and jacket along with a shirt and tie instead of his usual jeans and casual top.

"It was fine. Thank you for your help."

He nodded and a lock of hair fell across his forehead.

"I looked out for you on my way past, just in case. I took it as a good sign when your car wasn't there." Then he was gone, leaving Grace to deal with 30 pairs of curious eyes regarding her quizzically from their desks.

"Who was that, miss?" Sadie asked.

"Is he your boyfriend?" Callum chipped in and the entire classroom broke down into fits of laughter.

Yes, how ridiculous that Miss Anderson might have a boyfriend. Even Katie was smiling. In fact, Grace herself could feel her mouth curving upwards.

It was a ridiculous question, but Grace wouldn't have answered in any case. It wasn't appropriate to discuss her private life with her pupils.

"OK, everyone, that's enough. Let's settle down and we can talk about our holidays. Drama club starts back next week and I'll give you the details so anyone who's interested can come along."

## *Drama Group*

THE noise in the assembly hall was deafening as the pupils filed in at the end of lessons. A good number of faces new to the drama group were amongst them.

Grace stood on the stage with Lizzie and Ed and she smiled encouragingly as she spotted Katie creeping into the hall, though she was keeping her eyes averted, refusing to look at anyone.

Now she was here, Grace hoped the girl would begin to socialise with the other pupils in the group. She was pleased she'd managed to convince the teenager to come along this afternoon. It had taken some persuading.

"You won't have to join if you don't like it," she'd promised. "Just come along and see what it's about."

Katie had refused to meet her gaze.

"I'd rather die than get up on stage in front of everyone."

The girl's voice was so soft Grace had struggled to hear, but her heart had gone out to Katie.

"You don't need to perform unless you want to," she promised. "There are lots of other things you can become involved with. You could join me and the rest of the make-up team. Or help with scenery or costumes . . ."

"So I wouldn't have to do any acting at all?"

"Not if you don't want to. We all join in with the vocal exercises and physical stretches, and we all help with rehearsals, but not all of us want to be on stage."

She'd held her breath as she waited for Katie's decision, and when she gave the briefest of nods Grace could have whooped with delight. But she'd managed to stop herself. She didn't want to startle Katie before she'd even been to the first meeting.

"Great to see so many of you here!" Lizzie's voice was

raised above the noise. "Mr Price has some exciting news."

They waited as the noise level fell to a whisper and then to complete silence. Ed stepped to the front of the stage.

"Hi, everyone." He looked around with a grin. "As Miss Campbell mentioned, we have exciting plans for the group this year. We've been busy over the holidays and we've written a play we hope you'll like."

"We've prepared a list of characters, with a paragraph about each, so you can see if you'd like to audition for a part," Lizzie added. "We'll hand out copies later."

"There are twenty speaking parts in all," Ed added. "We can put some more of you on stage in non-speaking parts if you wish. And, as always, there are lots of jobs behind the scenes and front of house that we'll need help with."

"In addition, we're hoping to have a real-life theatre available for the end-of-year production," Lizzie told them.

There was a murmur as the pupils absorbed this. There could be few of them who didn't know about the plans to renovate the old theatre in town, but they would have had no idea Ed hoped to take the drama group there.

"It's early days, of course," Ed called over the chatting group. "But we very much hope the renovations will be finished in time."

The decibel level rose again as the implications sank in. They would be in a real theatre; on a real stage. This was the stuff of dreams for most of the budding young actors.

Hoping to see a similar excitement in Katie's expression, Grace glanced over to where the girl stood, a little apart from the others. But instead of anticipation, Grace was horrified to see only terror on the girl's face.

This had been a massive miscalculation. In trying to help Katie make friends and draw her out of herself, Grace had only succeeded in terrifying her. She was debating whether or not to go down to the floor to stand beside the girl when she saw Katie look at the door. She was going to bolt.

Grace had reached the bottom of the steps before Katie made a run for it. Without thinking, she broke into a sprint. She collided head on with Sean at the door.

"Hey," he teased, lifting his hands on to her arms to steady her. "Slow down or you'll do yourself an injury."

Winded, she paused for just a moment, glanced up into his blue eyes, then shook her head helplessly before running out of the door.

"Was it something I said?" he called after her and, without pausing or turning round, she lifted a hand in acknowledgement.

Where would Katie have gone? The girls' bathroom. That was as good a place to start the search as anywhere, and she knew she was on the right track when she heard snuffling from the far cubicle.

"Katie?" She knocked softly on the door. "It's Miss Anderson. Are you all right?"

She heard the lock slide open and the door opened to reveal a red-nosed Katie.

"I'm sorry, Miss Anderson. It was too much."

"It was a bit busy, wasn't it? We have twice the number that came last year. Word must be spreading."

Katie sniffed, then nodded.

"Everyone wants to be involved."

"Everyone apart from you?" Grace asked gently.

Katie looked up with large eyes.

"I do want to be involved," she protested. "It's just I don't like crowds. I don't feel I belong."

"Let's go to my classroom," Grace suggested. "We can have a proper chat in there."

"But don't you have to go back to the drama group?"

She placed a gentle arm around Katie's shoulders and began to guide her towards the Maths department.

"They can manage without us for a short while."

As Katie's registration teacher, Grace knew the year head

had been in touch with Katie's parents regarding the girl's shyness and lack of confidence. They had decided not to intervene – to allow Katie the chance to make friends in her own time, but that was obviously not going to happen without a little help.

"Now," she said to Katie as she led the way over to her desk and pulled up a chair for the girl. "How about we have a little sit down and compose ourselves, then maybe try to go back in for the end of the drama meeting?"

"Oh, but . . ."

"You wanted to be involved," Grace reminded her.

Katie sighed, then bit her lip and gave a tentative nod.

"Good. So let's talk over how we can make things a little easier for you. It's daunting to go to something as busy as the drama group on your own."

Grace paused. Katie had yet to make any friends amongst the other pupils, having joined school in second year. By then most friendships groups had already been firmly established and it was practically impossible for someone as timid as Katie to break in, however nice the others in her peer group might be.

Having lived in Montcraig all her life, Grace hadn't had to contend with anything like that. Yes, she'd had to meet new friends at university, but she'd been older and all the other students in her year had been new, too. So she couldn't imagine how difficult it must be for Katie.

Grace glanced at her watch.

"Why don't we go back and you can help me and the make-up crew?"

Katie made no response, but nodded.

"Thank you, Miss Anderson." She gave a half-hearted smile and she and Grace made their way back to the hall to join the others.

Sean made a beeline for her.

"Everything OK?" he asked.

She was cross with herself that she was so pleased to see him, and extra cross she was so pleased he seemed to care enough to check up on her.

"Yes, fine." She made an effort to hide her annoyance with herself by smiling. It wouldn't do to allow her tension to show in front of the pupils. "Katie and I are going to join the make-up crew."

She got Katie settled with a box of make-up, then caught Sean's eye and indicated she wanted to speak to him. She met him in an empty space in the middle of the hall.

"What are you doing here?"

He gave an easy grin.

"Ed asked if I'd help with scenery."

Typical Ed. But then he was only showing kindness to a new member of staff, including him, trying to make him feel involved in school life. She couldn't be cross about that, no matter how awkward it made life for her.

"What was going on with Katie?"

Briefly, she explained.

He nodded.

"I think she needs to be teamed up with someone who'll look out for her."

"We've tried." Grace sighed. "Most of the girls are lovely, but they just don't seem to be on the same wavelength."

Sean was thoughtful for a moment.

"What about the boys?"

"What about them?"

"Well, maybe Katie would be less intimidated by a boy. Boys are less complicated, they call a spade a spade."

"I don't know."

"What have we got to lose?"

Grace looked to where Katie was painfully sorting through the pots of make-up, purposefully avoiding eye contact with the other girls who made up the make-up crew.

"Did you have anyone in mind?"

"Callum Smith."

"What? He's loud and lively and he'd frighten the life out of her."

"He's outgoing and needs a steadying influence. They might be good for each other."

"And how do you propose we get them to be friends without making things awkward?"

"Let me take Katie to work on the scenery. We could use her help. She's in my art class and I've seen some of her work. She's very good. Callum's already helping me."

Grace felt very protective of Katie, but she knew they had to try to get her to interact with her peers. Being that insular really wasn't good for her.

"I suppose we could see how it goes."

"Do you want me to suggest it to her?"

Grace shook her head.

"No. I'll tell her what you said about being good at art and that you could use her help, then I'll send her over."

Before drama club finished that night, Katie and Callum were working nicely together planning out the scenery for one of the acts Lizzie and Ed had written into their play. Katie actually seemed happier than Grace had ever seen her.

Grace couldn't quite believe that Sean had found a solution that hadn't occurred to her or any of the other teachers who had expressed concern over Katie's withdrawn personality.

She revised her earlier opinion yet again. He hadn't just changed in the years he'd been away – he'd undergone a metamorphosis. It looked as though the carefree boy who only wanted to enjoy himself was now a fantastic teacher.

But, however much he'd changed, she still wasn't prepared to risk giving into the attraction that was undeniably still there. Chances were he was still bad boyfriend material.

# The Theatre

THE days passed by quickly and everyone settled into the routine of the new term. Before Sean knew it there was an autumn chill in the air and he was still no further forward in his quest to convince Grace to give him another chance.

"We get the keys tomorrow," Ed told him as he wandered into the art room.

"For the theatre?" Sean hazarded a wild guess. The theatre purchase had been the sole topic of conversation in town recently.

"What else?" Ed gave a short laugh as he pulled up a chair. "I'm actually really pleased it's all gone so smoothly."

Sean couldn't stop his sharp intake of breath.

"What?" Ed asked.

"Tempting fate?" Sean suggested and he put some paintbrushes away.

Ed laughed.

"I don't believe it! Sean McIver's superstitious."

"Maybe I am." Sean joined in the laughter. "I'm very impressed with all you've done, though. I can't believe how many people you convinced to get on board."

"It's a team effort. We couldn't have done it without the support of each and every name that's signed up to help."

Sean grinned.

"I'm sure every last one of us is grateful for all the work you've put in to pull this off."

Ed looked a little embarrassed at the praise.

"Grateful enough to put your name forward to join the committee?"

"Oh." So the reason for Ed's visit became crystal clear. "I don't know."

"Think about it," Ed urged.

"Is Grace putting her name forward."

Sean immediately recognised his mistake, but he hadn't been able to stop himself. Ed's eyebrows shot into his hairline. Thankfully he didn't say what was obviously on his mind.

"Yes. Yes, she is."

Sean nodded. The time for looking cool and blasé was well past.

"In that case, put me down, too."

"Sean, is that wise? I mean, you're a great guy and all, but should you really be chasing after Grace? You had your chance with her eight years ago and she's moved on."

He knew Ed was only looking out for Grace, but it still annoyed him. And even though Grace had assured him otherwise, he did wonder again if, maybe, Ed had more of an interest in Grace than a platonic friend might have.

"Am I treading on your toes or something?"

"Grace is a good friend and you hurt her badly last time."

No denial, Sean noted. And his words hit home. Sean knew he'd hurt Grace, but he didn't like hearing it from everyone. And he'd been hurt, too. Yes, it had been him who had left, but she had been the one who'd refused to go with him.

"I'm not interested in hurting her again."

Ed nodded slowly.

"Good. Well, it's great you're on board to help with the project."

Sean nodded. Regardless of Grace's involvement, this was something worth doing. Being involved would give him a chance to become involved in the community he was so desperate to re-establish himself in. Of course, Grace being there would be a bonus, but he would have volunteered regardless.

"We'll be looking for people to help with the practical

side of the renovations, too – clearing the place out, decorating and such."

He was tempted to once again ask if Grace was going to be involved, but all that would achieve would be to elicit another warning to keep away.

He smiled.

"Sounds like we're going to be busy."

Ed grinned.

"Thanks, I'll put your name down for the renovations."

"I really don't want to hurt her, you know," he called as Ed headed for the door.

The other man turned and looked at Sean for a moment, then slowly nodded.

"And she's a grown woman. I know you're just looking out for her, but she's perfectly capable of looking after herself."

Ed nodded again.

"You're right, of course. Forget I said anything."

&ast; &ast; &ast; &ast;

Sean was looking forward to getting started, but was startled by the reality of how much there was to do. Only half of the promised number of volunteers had turned out to help with the practical side of things.

The committee members were there, although Carol Parker, the architect, and both solicitors, Edward and Steve, made it clear they were there in an advisory capacity only and wouldn't be involved in the fetching and carrying.

"Everyone's busy at this time of year," Ed offered apologetically as he glanced around at the sorry turnout. "But more have promised to join us in the New Year."

Sean didn't really care about the others. He didn't care how hard he'd have to work or how long it would take. All he cared about was that being involved with this project would give him more time with Grace. Suddenly he hoped those extra volunteers wouldn't materialise, because if this was the only way he could spend time with her outside of school, he never wanted the work to end.

Grace had never been shy of hard work, but even she was daunted at the prospect of the task ahead. Clearing and updating a vast building like the old theatre seemed an impossible task.

Although, in the absence of any better offers, she should be grateful for the distraction. There were only so many coffees she could share with Lizzie and only so many programmes she could watch on television. And, with her parents still away, aside from marking and the drama group, there would be very little else to do in town over the dark winter evenings.

"I'm not looking forward to this," Lizzie whispered in her ear. "Looks like he's expecting us all to get involved with the heavy physical work."

Grace smiled.

"It will keep us fit," she pointed out, trying to find an angle that would appeal to her friend. "And it will be cheaper than joining a gym."

Lizzie laughed and brought Ed's attention over to them, but he didn't say anything. Grace noticed his gaze linger on Lizzie's face for a moment longer than it should, but then he carried on with his troops' rousing talk.

"We aim to have the theatre up and running in time for Montcraig High's drama production in June," Ed told them. "That gives us plenty of time to get the place up to scratch."

"It sounds like a long time, but it will fly by," someone in the corner shouted and there was a general murmur of agreement.

"So, there's lots to do, but if we all pitch in we can do it," Ed told them.

"I've never noticed how attractive he is when he's being

all masterful," Lizzie whispered. Grace was sure it was supposed to be a joke, but the way her friend was looking at Ed made her think there might be something more to it.

She hoped she was right. Maybe they only needed a little helping hand to push things along. And she'd always fancied playing Cupid . . .

"Probably best if we split into teams to start with," Ed suggested. "That way we can each tackle an area without getting under each other's feet. Carol is going to allocate you all to different areas, so if you see her then we can all get started."

Somehow Grace was paired up with Sean. She toyed with the idea of objecting, of demanding to be paired with someone else, but realised it would seem childish. Besides, she found she didn't mind half as much as she should have.

They were given some refuse sacks and despatched to the office. Not the box office – that would have been too easy. They were sent to the general office, which was well out of the way.

Grace was out of breath by the time they'd climbed up three flights of stairs. Then she looked suspiciously at the tiny, rickety set of stairs they'd have to negotiate to go up another level to the top of the theatre.

"It doesn't look very safe," she told Sean as she peered up into the dark.

"The building was properly surveyed before we bought it," he pointed out reasonably and fished in the pocket of his jacket for a small torch. He swung the beam around and soon found the light switch for the narrow set of stairs. "If there was anything to worry about, it would have shown up on the report."

Grace knew what he said was true, yet she still couldn't bring herself to step on to that first wooden tread. Now it was lit, the flight looked even more forbidding then it had in complete darkness.

"It's safe. I promise," Sean said, his voice a whisper in her ear. "Come on, let's go and see just how much work we have to do up there."

He held out his hand, and she hesitated for a moment before she took it in her own. His fingers folded around hers, his touch warm and reassuring. Suddenly she felt she could take on the world.

"OK." She nodded. "Let's go."

He led the way, not letting go of her hand even when they reached the top. She found it was just a room up there. An impossibly messy room with piles of papers and dusty old books reaching from floor to ceiling.

Grace felt a mild panic as she looked around. It would probably take the two of them between now and Ed's deadline of June to make the tiniest dent in this lot.

"What are we going to do with it?" she asked, her voice hardly more than a croak.

He didn't reply immediately. Instead, he waved the roll of black bin bags he'd brought up and let go of her so he could comb the fingers of his other hand through his hair as he looked around the room.

"Do what Ed told us, I suppose," he said at last. "Go through it all and throw out as much as we can."

Still slightly shocked, she nodded as she spun around again, hoping that, by some miracle, things might not be quite as bad as they'd seemed at first. If anything, at second glance, they were worse.

"We'd best get on with it, I suppose, and get as much as we can done." They didn't have long. Ed had already said they would all leave at ten this evening. Most people had work in the morning and he didn't want people dropping out of the project because they were being worked too hard. "We've only got a couple of hours tonight."

Grace reached out and took the bin bags from him, ignoring the shock of awareness that ran up her arm as their fingers brushed.

"Here." She tore the first bag off and handed it to him. "You get started on the desk and I'll try to clear this pile in the corner."

Luckily she was wearing her oldest jeans, so she didn't think twice about sitting on the floor with a handful of the papers.

"Invoices," she muttered. "And statements. All nearly thirty years old. No point keeping these." She put the papers she'd checked into a bag.

"Same here." Sean absently dropped some papers into his own bag. "Do you know, I don't think anyone's been up here in all the time this place was a bingo hall."

"You're probably right. I don't think they ever went farther than the ground floor. They took the original seats out from the stalls to make way for the bingo tables, but the original seats are still in the circle and balcony."

Sean nodded.

"Yes, I noticed that when we looked around the other day. So much wasted space."

That was why it was so important they made a good job of clearing the place. Now it belonged to the community they needed to make sure every inch of space was used properly.

They worked in silence for a while, Grace doing her best not to glance over every five seconds. He drew her gaze with an invisible force, which wasn't surprising because he was still the most gorgeous man she'd ever seen. Working alone with him in the far reaches of the theatre, away from the others, was an intensely intimate experience and she was struggling to keep things professional. Particularly after the casual way he'd held her hand earlier.

"Your idea to encourage Callum to take Katie under his wing seems to have worked well," she said when she couldn't stand the silence a moment longer.

"Looks like they're getting to be good friends," he agreed.

"He was always a bit on the wild side," Grace continued as she carried on through the pile of paperwork. "But Katie's calmed him down, and he's given her some confidence. It actually used to break my heart to see her on her own all the time, trying not to be noticed. But she's forging other friendships now, too."

"That's what I hoped would happen. There was a similar situation at my last school. One child who was painfully introverted, another who was over-exuberant. It all worked out well in the end."

"Did you like your last school?" As she watched he looked across.

"Yes, very much."

"In that case, why did you leave?"

His blue eyes were fixed to her face, unflinching. She wanted to look away but couldn't.

"I thought it was time I came home."

"Montcraig hasn't been your home for a long time, Sean."

For the longest moment he was quiet. His gaze was fierce and she thought she'd made him angry. Then his face softened into the faintest of smiles.

"But they say home is where the heart is, Grace."

# *Playing Cupid*

"ARE you absolutely sure Ed doesn't have designs on you?"

Grace looked up from the pile of papers she was sifting through and laughed before realising Sean was serious.

"What?"

"He seems very attentive."

"To me? Oh, no, Sean, you've got it completely wrong."

"Are you going to tell me you're just old friends?"

"Yes," she said. "Very much so."

The significance wasn't lost on her – that was how she'd described her relationship with Sean when Harriet had queried the situation. Yet she'd exchanged enough meaningful glances with Sean since they started working at the theatre that they both now realised there was definitely something there.

"Really," she insisted. "We are just friends."

Sean looked at her for a long moment and her heart gave a little flutter. There was definitely something there, however much she tried to deny it. Then he broke the connection and turned back to his own pile of old letters and invoices.

"He warned me off you."

"What?"

"He doesn't want you getting hurt."

Grace felt her face redden. Ed being friendly was one thing, but meddling in her relationship with Sean was a step too far for any friend.

"He had no right."

Sean shrugged.

"He was looking out for you. But I did wonder if there was more to it."

"Definitely not. I've already told you, I've never been interested in him that way. And he's never been interested in me."

"You're sure."

"Of course I'm sure. Why would he even look at me twice when he's desperately in love with Lizzie." Grace immediately clamped her hand over her mouth. "Oh."

Sean swung round.

"It's Lizzie he's interested in," he said almost to himself. "Well, that makes sense."

"That's a secret," Grace told him. "You must promise not to tell anyone."

He raised an eyebrow.

"I thought we were supposed to be teachers, not school children."

"But Lizzie doesn't know."

Sean looked at her as though she was crazy.

"Why doesn't he tell her?"

"He doesn't want to scare her off."

"It's funny," he said, "how you can see how daft your own behaviour is when you see someone else making the same mistakes."

Grace felt something snap exactly where her heart was. What exactly was he trying to say?

"Don't tell me you're in love with Lizzie, too?" Her voice was a horrified squeak.

Had she misread the situation enough to mistake Sean's interest in her, when all the time it had been Lizzie he found attractive? She'd been telling herself ever since he'd arrived back in town that she was most definitely not interested in Sean in any romantic capacity, but now she found she wasn't remotely pleased to suspect he might be interested in someone else.

He grinned.

"Oh, Grace. Don't be so silly."

She didn't know whether she should be cross he'd called her silly, or relieved he didn't find Lizzie attractive. She decided to go with relieved.

"So you're not in love with Lizzie?"

"Of course not, but I do think Ed should tell her how he feels."

"I've told him so, but it has to be his decision. We can't force him into a confession."

"Perhaps not. But we could maybe offer a little encouragement."

"What do you have in mind?" Grace asked.

"You and I take Lizzie and Ed out for dinner on Saturday night, just to see where it all goes."

"You mean like some sort of double date or something?" Grace couldn't prevent the scornful tone from slipping into her voice. It was he who'd mentioned they were supposed to be teachers, and a double date to set friends up seemed very like teenage behaviour to her.

"Not exactly. Just the four of us having dinner to relax after a very long week." He paused and looked around and Grace followed his gaze. There was still a lot of work to do here in the general office, but they'd already taken countless bags of old papers to the recycling centre and they were beginning to see a difference.

"We have worked hard," she agreed.

They hadn't stopped for the past two weeks. The group of volunteers had turned up at six each evening after work and had worked through until ten. They had weeks of this ahead of them, although Ed had suggested they take the following week off. He didn't want them all becoming tired and fed up of the project. Besides, a number of the teachers, including Grace and Sean, were taking the pupils to London on an arts trip.

"Shall I suggest it? It won't be a late night as we all have to get packed and catch up with our own errands on Sunday, but it might give Ed the push he needs to suggest to Lizzie they could go out on their own some time."

Grace doubted it would work. Over the years she'd known Lizzie, Ed had been in her company countless times. It was unlikely anything would be different this time. But she didn't want to be too negative when Sean was trying to be helpful. Besides, whatever the outcome, it was bound to be a good evening and Grace quite fancied a night out with her three closest friends.

That gave her a jolt. Sean was one of her closest friends. It had taken the suggestion of a meal out with Ed and Lizzie to make her realise she wanted to be there with Sean more than she did with the other two. How had that happened? She'd been so adamant she wasn't going to allow him to break through her defences.

"I think it's worth a go," she told him.

Sean nodded, then gave a low whistle as he shuffled through a box he'd pulled from one of the desks.

"What is it?" Grace asked.

"Come over and see."

Grace peered over his shoulder and breathed in sharply. In the box Sean had uncovered was a complete history of the old theatre in the years before it had become a bingo hall. Someone had collected together programmes, unused tickets, photographs and precious memorabilia from the shows that had been staged here.

"Looks like some of these go back years," she said.

"And there are photos and programmes right up until the theatre closed in the Eighties," he added. "This is phenomenal. Can you imagine what this lot would be worth to a collector?"

Grace was aghast.

"You can't sell them," she told him. "They might belong to someone."

"I'm guessing they belong to the theatre," he said. "In

which case they now belong to the community, and the community will be looking to fund-raise over the next few months as we try to get the place up to standard."

"I don't know. I think we should try to find out who they belong to. They might be part of a private collection. We can't just sell them without checking."

Sean was a bit annoyed to say the least, and he was sure it showed.

"Do you honestly think I'd try to sell this stuff without trying to find out the legal position with ownership?"

As he watched her, he was pleased to see she flushed a deep red. At least she was embarrassed to have made the accusations.

"I didn't think. I mean . . . I'm sorry Sean. But you were going on about how much it was all worth and how much it would help the theatre."

"I'll bring it all before the committee. Maybe we can set up a meeting before dinner on Saturday." Although he wasn't entirely sure he wanted any part of any dinner anymore, even if it had all been his idea. He was gutted Grace could think him capable of theft.

"That's a good idea." Her brown eyes were distressed and his heart melted a little and he realised it wasn't her fault. He'd been so excited about the find it was understandable she might have mistaken his intentions.

"I still can't get the idea out of my head that someone who worked here saved a programme or a photo or ticket from each performance and we've stumbled on a personal collection."

He could see she was concerned. And, if her suspicions were proved correct, then it would have been unthinkable to do anything other than try to find the rightful owner. However, he still had his doubts.

"This lot was collected over many decades," he pointed out. "Possibly longer than a working lifetime."

She smiled.

"Of course, you're right."

"But we'll still get the committee to make enquiries before they decide what to do with the collection."

"I'm sorry, Sean. I should have known you'd want to do the right thing."

He forgave her instantly. How could he not? She stood there with her brown eyes huge and full of remorse, her blonde curls framing her lovely face, and he knew he'd forgive her anything. Even changing her mind about travelling with him and sending him away.

In fact, he'd forgiven her for that a long time ago.

"I'll have a word with Ed and tell him what we found. I'll suggest he tries to get everyone together on Saturday afternoon. That will make our suggestion of a dinner together easier to make."

"That's a good idea." She smiled and he could feel his own lips curve in response. She was still standing over him, looking into the box on the desk and he could smell her perfume. It would be so easy to get to his feet, to pull her into his arms and to kiss her.

But, no matter how foolish he though Ed for his silence where Lizzie was concerned, he found he shared the other man's fears exactly. Pushing the situation might frighten Grace away, and at least now he had her friendship. That had to be enough for now.

*　　　　*　　　　*　　　　*

By Saturday, Sean had catalogued the contents of the desk and performances going back many decades were carefully commemorated with a memento. He was pleased when Grace arrived early at the theatre to help him set it all up.

"You must have worked through the past two nights," she commented as she pulled a table into position.

He had, but it was worth it to see how impressed she was.

"I've never needed a lot of sleep." He grinned and was rewarded with a smile. "There are some duplicates: extra programmes, bundles of unused tickets. And the photographs can all be copied, so if the committee decide to sell some of them we wouldn't have to get rid of the originals."

"It's a very impressive collection," she told him as the others arrived for the meeting.

The committee was enthralled by the find.

"If they belong to the theatre, we could sell any duplicates of the programmes and copies of the photographs," Ed suggested. "Obviously, we'll take a vote, but I wouldn't want to split the collection or sell it. We need to find out where we stand first, though."

Sean turned to the two solicitors.

"Edward, Steve, can we leave it to you two to make enquiries?"

They both nodded their agreement and the meeting broke up shortly after that. Everyone was tired and keen to get away to start their free week after all the hard work they'd been putting into the theatre.

"You two ready?" Sean asked Lizzie and Ed and they nodded. He noticed Lizzie held back to walk out to the car park with Grace.

"What's going on?" he heard her whisper.

"Nothing," Grace assured her. "We just thought it would be nice to end the week with a meal out."

"You're not falling under his spell again?"

He held his breath as he waited for Grace to reply. He knew he should make them aware he could overhear, but he was paralysed by his desire to hear the answer he hoped she'd utter.

"Of course not," Grace replied.

Sean felt the crushing blow of disappointment. He didn't realise until just that moment exactly how much he'd hoped

Grace was falling under his spell. They'd been getting on so well this past week. Not quite as they had before he'd left Montcraig, but it could easily build to that, he was sure. Now, though, Grace denied feeling anything for him.

It was a disappointment he could have done without.

"So, shall we go in one car?" Ed asked.

"Best take two," Sean answered. "I've got art supplies in the back of mine. The canvases wouldn't fit in the boot."

The excuse was genuine and Ed took it as such.

"Grace, do you want to come with me?"

"Actually, it's probably best if I go with Sean," she replied and was treated to suspicious glances from the other two. "We need to discuss where we're at with clearing that office," she rushed to explain.

That wasn't too far from the truth. All they'd been talking about recently was the office at the theatre. The papers they'd uncovered were fascinating – even for maths and art teachers who had no interest in history.

Ed didn't look happy about the plan. Neither did Lizzie.

"You sure, honey?" she asked Grace.

"Of course. Everything's fine between us now so there's nothing to worry about. You go off with Ed and Sean and I will follow."

Reluctantly, Lizzie did as Grace suggested.

"That didn't go too well," she said when they were on their way.

"She wasn't as enthusiastic as I'd hoped," Sean admitted.

"Neither was Ed enthusiastic," Grace said. "He's terrified of saying the wrong thing if he spends too much time with Lizzie."

"Maybe the wrong thing is what's needed."

"I don't know, Sean."

"Well, we'll see how it goes. If they're still unhappy when they arrive at the restaurant, then I'll give Lizzie a lift back."

Grace frowned.

"What is it?" Sean asked.

"One journey's probably not going to be long enough. Ed is shy around Lizzie, and Lizzie doesn't have a clue how he feels. Maybe we should give them the journey back either way to try and sort it out."

Sean felt hope surge in his heart at that suggestion. If Grace was so adamant they needed to give Lizzie and Ed more time alone together, then it followed she didn't completely object to spending time with him. Yes, they'd been working together closely over the past few weeks. Between the drama group and the theatre and the times they bumped into each other at school, they were hardly apart. But those times were based on necessity and circumstances and were not easily avoided.

She could have avoided this if she'd wanted. She could have gone with Ed and Lizzie. But she'd decided she preferred to go to the restaurant with him.

He knew he was probably reading too much into it, but he couldn't help thinking it might be a good sign.

\*　　　　\*　　　　\*　　　　\*

The meal went well. They talked shop, but they also laughed a lot, too.

The starter and main course passed almost without Grace noticing. Even though she knew this was a ploy to get Lizzie and Ed together, she was actually enjoying herself. In fact, she had to keep reminding herself that this wasn't really an evening for her and Sean, so easy had she become in his company.

With that realisation came an insistent throbbing behind her left eye. A migraine attack was imminent. She needed to go home fast so she could take her medication and lie down before it became unbearable.

Of course, the timing couldn't have been better in terms

of allowing Lizzie and Ed time alone, because she was going to have to ask Sean to take her home sooner rather than later.

When the waiter brought the dessert menu, she declined, as did Sean.

"Do you mind if I have cake?" Lizzie asked. "I live for pudding and the chocolate fudge cake here is to die for."

"Go ahead," Ed invited. "In fact, I might join you."

And that was when Grace decided to leave the potential lovebirds to it. She and Sean wouldn't hang around and hold their hands for ever. They had to be left alone to see if a romance might flourish between the two, or if they were destined to stay for ever in the friend zone.

She looked at Sean and just for a moment she forgot what she was going to say.

He smiled and she returned the gesture.

"OK?" he asked.

She nodded.

"Although I think I feel a migraine coming on."

Sean did the gentlemanly thing, just as she'd expected he would. He might have run out on her when she'd needed him before, but since he'd returned his manners had been faultless. He fetched her coat and draped it around her shoulders before guiding her to her feet.

"You sure you two don't mind?" Grace asked as she picked up her handbag. "I hate to ruin the evening, but if I stay I'll only make you all miserable."

Lizzie looked concerned.

"Shall I come with you?"

"Thanks, but you stay and have your cake. Sean will take me home and I'll take a couple of tablets when I get in and I'll be right as rain in the morning."

"I'll be round in the morning to see how you are, and to help with your packing if you need it," Lizzie offered.

Grace wasn't about to turn her down. Not that she needed

any help with her packing, but she would want to know if anything had developed between her and Ed.

"That would be great," Grace accepted. "Thank you. Not too early, though. I'm intending to have a bit of a lie in. I'm going to need all my energies for next week."

Ed rubbed his chin.

"I don't see how a Maths teacher has ended up going on the arts trip."

"They needed volunteers, and it isn't as though there are any Maths trips I need to help out on," she told him.

Ed nodded, then they said their goodbyes and she and Sean left.

"How do you think it went?" she asked Sean when they got into his car.

"As well as could be expected." He glanced over and grinned. "Let's hope they get a bit cosier with us out of the way. Otherwise they won't ever get together."

"I think they might be too far into the friend zone already," Grace confided.

"You might be right, but never let it be said we haven't done our best."

There was one thing Grace wasn't sure about, though.

"Why are you so interested in Lizzie and Ed getting together?"

His smiled took her breath away.

"I feel empathy for Ed. There's a girl I'm keen on, but I know if I tell her she'd go into retreat and I'll lose the friendship we have now."

Despite her growing discomfort with her migraine and the fact she'd told him there was no hope, Grace knew he was talking about her.

She said nothing. Even though they'd been getting on so well recently – and even though when she looked at him, she knew she still had feelings for him – she couldn't bring herself to say the words that would offer him hope.

68

## *School Trip*

GRACE was cold, still half asleep and her head foggy from the after-effects of her migraine as she drove into the school car park on Monday morning. She managed to force her brain to think of the week ahead as she pulled her suitcase from the boot. She even managed a smile as Lizzie approached and they walked together towards the waiting bus.

"We kissed," Lizzie revealed in a hushed whisper. "Ed and I kissed!"

Grace stopped mid-stride and dropped her suitcase on to the damp tarmac. Open mouthed, she swung around to face her friend.

"You didn't!"

Lizzie's expression mirrored Grace's surprise.

"I know! I couldn't believe it either."

"Did this happen on Saturday night?" Grace had cancelled Lizzie's planned visit yesterday – her migraine had made her incapable of socialising with anyone.

Lizzie nodded.

"He took me home after you and Sean left the restaurant and he walked me to my door. I don't know quite what happened, but I couldn't help myself. I pounced on him." Lizzie's blush was so bright that it was unmistakeable, even in the poor morning light. "I kissed him senseless and didn't give him a chance to object."

This was what she and Sean had both hoped for, but Grace had never really expected it to happen.

"I knew you were perfect for each other, but I didn't even think you liked him that way."

"Me neither. I don't know what made me realise. Maybe it was seeing how he's been taking charge of the theatre project. Or maybe it was because of how well you and Sean were getting on and it made me wonder if Ed and I could ever be that close."

"Sean and I aren't close. Not these days."

Grace winced from the sceptical flash in Lizzie's eyes.

"Are you sure?"

"Positive," she insisted. "You know how things are between me and Sean."

"Yes," Lizzie agreed. "But you seem to have been getting on rather well recently."

"We're colleagues and friends. There's no more to be said. But I want to know more about you and Ed. I can't believe you're telling me all about it now when I'm about to get on a bus headed for London. Why didn't you say when I rang you to cancel yesterday?"

Lizzie shrugged.

"I needed to get it straight in my own head before I spoke about it. Besides, I know what you're like when you get one of your heads. You have to be left alone in a darkened room and too much excitement would have set you back."

"True." She nodded. "And have you? Got it straight, I mean."

"I think so."

Grace was aware of pupils and teachers milling around and was annoyed she wouldn't be able to have the proper chat she wanted.

"We'll have to meet up when I get back. Have a proper catch up."

"I'd like that."

"So, tell me quickly before I have to get on this coach, what do you want to happen?"

Lizzie bit her lip then smiled.

"I think I want to go out with him again and see where it leads."

"And has Ed said anything?"

Lizzie's smile was dazzling.

"He's asked me to go to the pictures tonight."

Grace boarded the coach and slipped into her seat beside Sean.

"Your plan seems to have worked." He raised an eyebrow and Grace explained.

"Sounds like Ed didn't need to pluck up any kind of courage," he commented thoughtfully.

"No," Grace agreed. "It seems Lizzie reached the decision without any kind of prompting."

"Well, I hope it works out for them."

"Me, too. They're both so lovely and they deserve to be happy. I think they're perfect for each other. I can't wait to hear Ed's take on it. He must have been so surprised when Lizzie kissed him."

Sean laughed softly at her side and a shiver ran down Grace's spine. He had a nice laugh. She wished he'd laugh more often.

The journey passed without incident and before they knew it they were checking into their hotel. Grace was sharing with Marie, one of the art teachers, and they quickly got settled in before heading out to make sure the female pupils on the trip were happy with their rooms and behaving in line with school policy.

"How are you doing, Katie?" Grace asked the quiet pupil who had settled into a room with two other girls.

"Fine, thank you, Miss Anderson," Katie said, her voice barely audible, but she smiled brightly from where she was perched on one of the beds with her two classmates.

Grace was so pleased to see the change in the girl. She was a different child to the one who had started the term in Grace's registration class.

Grace knew she had Sean to thank for that. Katie and Callum had formed a strong friendship, and from that Katie had gained confidence and was now making tentative steps towards forging relationships with other pupils. Just as Sean had expected she would.

Grace was smiling as she made her way to meet with the other teachers.

They had a busy few days planned. They were taking a tour of the city, Sean had arranged a West End show and they were hoping to squeeze in a visit to a couple of museums and art galleries. Grace had been looking forward to it since she'd volunteered and was pleased the group of pupils they had brought were well behaved and not likely to cause trouble.

"Everyone settled in?" Sean asked as Grace joined him downstairs in the restaurant.

"All fine." She smiled. "Everyone's raring to go."

"Good." He smiled again and, as their eyes met, Grace experienced the most unsettling feeling.

She quickly checked herself. She mustn't allow herself to travel down that path again. She knew Sean was interested and he was just too charming for comfort, but she desperately needed to strengthen her armour and fix it in place to protect her heart.

They split into smaller parties and Grace found herself paired off with Sean as their group moved around the various galleries.

The trip was an education for her. She was enthralled as she listened to Sean impart knowledge of painting and she was carried along by his passion for talent and beauty.

"You're really good at this," she told him as they brought up the rear of their small party.

He seemed surprised by her words.

"Thank you. I didn't expect that from you."

"Why ever not?"

"Well." He glanced around to make sure there was nobody within earshot. "You seem to be very careful not to offer me any encouragement these days."

That threw her. She hadn't expected him to get so personal. She looked at him and nearly melted on the spot. But she knew she had to keep strong.

"I don't quite know what to say, Sean."

He smiled a little sadly.

"You're not denying it."

"I used to think you were pretty wonderful until you ruined it all by leaving."

"You were supposed to come with me."

She drew in a sharp breath at the reminder.

"Sean, I don't think this is the time or the place to talk about this." She looked around for the pupils in their group, eager for some distraction. The last time she'd begun to relax in his company she'd ended up with a migraine. She certainly didn't want a repetition of that.

"You're right," he agreed with a heavy sigh. "But, if we're to move forward at all, we have to find a time and a place to talk. Things have been OK between us these past few weeks and there's no reason they can't get even better. If that's what we both want."

Even though she'd made it pretty obvious she wasn't keen, Sean knew he would have to speak to Grace and sort things out. Despite his earlier decision to leave the matter well alone he knew they couldn't carry on like this. And he had cause to hope, because even though she'd said she wasn't interested, the way she'd looked at him a moment ago told a different tale.

She'd looked at him the way she had used to. A way that made his breath catch in his chest.

She had been right when she'd told him this wasn't the time, though. They were responsible for a group of teenagers and personal issues had no place here. He fully intended to enjoy this trip and to enjoy Grace's company. Without pressure and without thinking about any other issues to complicate matters.

But when they got back to Montcraig it would be a different matter.

"OK, everyone," Sean called to the pupils. "We need to make our way back so we can go for lunch."

The pupils all filed out of the gallery and Grace performed a quick head count to make sure they were all there.

It was only as they were preparing to leave the restaurant that they noticed anything amiss.

"Mr McIver." One of the boys came up to Sean with a concerned frown. "I'm worried about Callum. He went to use the bathroom earlier and he's still not back."

Well accustomed to the teenage tendency to over-dramatise every situation, Sean wasn't overly concerned.

"When did he go?"

"Almost as soon as the main course was served."

OK, that had been quite a while ago. Maybe there was cause for concern, after all.

"Have you been to see if he's OK?"

"I'll go now."

The boy dashed off and soon returned, looking worried.

"He's not there."

This was all Sean needed. Things had gone so well up until now and for this to happen on their last day was not good.

"Well, we can't go home without him, so we'd better hope he turns up."

"Katie's gone, too," a wide-eyed Sadie Simpson confided.

Sean resisted the urge to panic. He took a deep breath.

"Do you have any idea where?"

The girl shook her head.

"They're probably together," Grace suggested softly.

Sean immediately felt a pang of guilt. He had been the one to suggest Callum and Katie might get on and he was horrified at the thought it was his fault this had happened. He had expected Katie to be a calming influence on

Callum, and for Callum to bring Katie out of her shell. But it looked as though, instead of providing a steadying influence, Katie had danced over to the wild side with her new friend.

"I think we'd better start asking questions," Grace continued. "And maybe we should think about contacting the police."

It turned out Katie had been rather taken with a painting of a young couple in a gallery they'd visited that morning.

"It was all she talked about," Sadie said.

"Do you think she might have persuaded Callum to go back for another look?" Grace suggested. "Perhaps we'll find them there."

"As it's our only lead, it's certainly worth a shot."

He took Grace with him, leaving the pupils with the other teachers, and hailed a cab.

"What if they're not there?" Grace asked, worrying at her lower lip.

"Let's think positively." He knew he sounded brighter than he felt, but he didn't want her to worry more than she already was.

"You don't think they might have run away together?" Her voice was a frightened whisper, and he knew exactly why. The thought they might have lost two of their pupils was unthinkable.

"Of course they haven't." He sounded a lot more confident than he felt.

She sighed.

"But . . ." Her voice trailed off.

"If they're not at the gallery, then we'll call the police."

She nodded, her blonde curls bobbing around her shoulders as she did so. He was tempted to reflect on how well it looked, but he forced himself to focus. There were bigger issues to worry about than how lovely Grace's hair was in the sunlight. If their pupils weren't at the gallery, then he would have no clue where to start looking for them.

Grace sighed again and rested her hand on his hand. This was the first time since his return that she'd voluntarily touched him. For a brief moment he could think of nothing else as the heat from her fingers warmed his skin.

"You're right. They'll be there," she told him. "I'm sure they will. They're both sensible young people. They won't have done anything daft."

They were at the gallery within minutes. Dread rushed through him and made him dizzy when Katie and Callum were nowhere to be seen. The area in front of the painting Sadie had mentioned was deserted.

He heard Grace's soft sigh of disappointment and he wanted to put his arm around her and comfort her. She looked as worried as he felt.

"We'd better call the police," he said softly, but she wasn't listening. She was looking past him towards the gift shop and, when he followed her gaze, he recognised a red coat and a black jacket and two dark-haired teenagers.

"They're in the gift shop," she muttered and began to march with purpose towards the runaways. "What do you two think you're doing?" she demanded. He recognised the snappy tone of someone elevated from concern to relief. "We've all been worried sick about you!"

"Miss Anderson!" Katie exclaimed, a frightened expression crossing her face. "Mr McIver. I'm sorry, we didn't mean to cause any trouble."

"You shouldn't have run away," Grace said a little more gently.

"We didn't run away," Callum broke in. "We just wanted to come back to the gift shop. We thought we'd make it back before anyone missed us."

"Fortunately you have friends who look out for you," Sean said, his own tone every bit as serious as Grace's had been. Anything could have happened, they could have gone anywhere and, as the teacher responsible for their group, it would all have been his fault. "What was so urgent that you had to rush back here?"

"This." Katie held up a postcard, a soft blush warming her cheeks. "Callum wanted to buy me this, because he knew how much I loved the painting."

Sean looked at the postcard. It was a depiction of the painting Katie had loved so much.

Sean shook his head. It was sweet that Callum had brought Katie all the way back here to buy a memento of something she loved, but he had to make them understand what they'd done today wasn't acceptable behaviour.

"You can't take off whenever you want," he reminded them.

"We didn't mean any harm." Callum raised his voice and other visitors to the gift shop looked on with interest.

Sean realised they were getting nowhere and he raised an eyebrow at the boy and watched him squirm. Sean had learned early in his teaching career that there was hardly any need for a teacher to shout. A look was, for the most part, enough.

"We'll talk about this when we get back to school," he said quietly. "But you'd better get your story ready because you'll have to explain yourselves to Mrs Roberts. And to your parents."

At that point, Katie began to cry. Sean wasn't happy. He wasn't in the habit of upsetting his pupils, but he had to impress on the two of them the seriousness of their leaving the group without permission. They'd caused a lot of unnecessary worry to the teachers and to the other pupils and they couldn't be allowed to carry on thinking that kind of thoughtlessness had any place on a school excursion.

"Come on, Katie." Grace handed out a tissue and placed an arm about the girl's shoulder. "Let's get you and Callum back to the others."

The bus was waiting for them as they got out of their cab and everyone was already on board. Thankfully, Katie had stopped crying and reluctantly climbed up the steps, followed by Callum.

She and Sean heard a cheer rise up from the other pupils as the two made their way to their seats.

"Everyone seems pleased to see them back," Sean commented with a smile.

Grace worried at her lower lip.

"Sean, do you think we were too hard on them? After all, they only went back to buy a postcard."

"They left the group without permission and without telling anyone where they were going," Sean reminded her. "We can't allow that to happen without punishment, or next time there's a trip there'll be pandemonium."

She knew he was right. But the thought of how upset Katie had been worried her.

She nodded.

"Maybe I'll have a word with Katie on the journey back to make sure she's OK."

"Good idea. Although I think we'd better join the others on the coach. Looks like they're waiting for us."

Grace looked up to find a collection of curious faces pressed against the glass of the coach windows. She gave a smile and a little wave, then followed Sean on board and took her seat next to him at the front.

She was looking forward to getting home. Looking forward to her own bed and her own bathroom in her own flat. Much as she'd enjoyed the trip, it had reiterated how much of a homebody she really was. Maybe it was just as well Sean had travelled the world without her, because they really were so unsuited.

## A Late-night Visitor

"SO." Lizzie sat back with a jangle of her bangles and stared hard at Grace. "What happened on the trip? How did you get on with Sean?"

Grace laughed.

"Stop trying to deflect the spotlight from you. I want to know what's happened with you and Ed. Last I heard you seemed to be getting on rather well."

Lizzie smiled.

"Things are going swimmingly."

"Good." Grace couldn't stop herself from grinning. "And what happened to never getting involved again?"

Lizzie had been married in the dim and distant past. A youthful mistake, she always said whenever asked, but Grace knew the experience had hurt her deeply. She suspected it was the reason for her blind spot when it came to realising how perfect Ed was for her.

"Maybe I think Ed's worth risking a broken heart for."

Grace smiled. This was what she'd wanted for her friends.

"Ed's not going to break your heart," she told Lizzie. "He's a lovely man and he thinks the world of you."

"Yes, well, I hope you're right. Anyway, we should discuss Christmas. Then I want to hear all about the trip."

"What about Christmas?" This had all been settled months ago. Lizzie normally joined Grace and her parents for the big day, but, knowing Annie and Alistair Anderson were going to be away this year, the girls had made plans to spend the day together.

"I wondered . . ." Lizzie looked at her with huge eyes ". . . how you'd feel if I invited Ed to join us?"

"Great idea," Grace said. And it was. If Lizzie was thinking of sharing such an important day with him, things with Ed must have gone even better than she'd suspected.

"And . . ."

Grace instantly got a bad feeling.

"What?" she asked suspiciously.

"Well, I spoke to Sean and he says he's staying in town for the holidays. But he's going to be on his own."

"So you want to ask him, too?" So much for things looking up, with Ed and his invitation for Christmas Day marking him out as special. It seemed Lizzie was intent on inviting all the strays from Montcraig High to share the big day with them.

Lizzie nodded.

"If you don't mind."

"Why would I mind?" Grace said, a little too quickly. "It's got nothing to do with me. You're the one who offered to host Christmas lunch. If you're OK with cooking for another person, why would I object?"

"You're sure?"

Grace nodded.

"Absolutely."

"All right, then. I'll ask him."

Grace resisted the urge to show any emotion other than mild curiosity about what the day might bring them. But, even though she'd never admit it out loud, she thought Lizzie had done the right thing. The thought of Sean being alone at Christmas wasn't a pleasant one.

She would turn up on Christmas Day, armed with gifts and wearing a big smile and she would do her best to enjoy the day. After all, there was no reason not to – all three were friends of hers. And even if Sean's presence always made her heart beat a little faster, she would just jolly well have to ignore it.

"So, tell me," Lizzie persisted. "How did you get on with Sean on the trip?"

"Yeah, it was all fine." Grace told her about the near miss

with losing two pupils and Lizzie laughed when she heard about the havoc they'd caused by going to buy a postcard, of all things.

"It's not funny," she protested. "We had to get a cab and chase around all over the place looking for them."

"At least they're both safe and well. You worry too much."

"I don't think I worried enough," Grace told her. How could you worry too much about somebody else's children when they were in your care? She suppressed a shudder when she thought about what might have happened to the two teenagers as they crossed a busy city they weren't accustomed to on their own. "Besides, you're a fine one to talk," she reminded Lizzie. "You worry about your pupils just as much as I do."

"True, but in this case I'm sure I would have let it go by now. They're both safe. Everyone's fine. They've learned they can't go off when they're supposed to be with the group and they won't do it next time."

Grace nodded.

"You're right, of course, but I am worried about the effect it might have on Katie. She was so quiet and withdrawn. Callum has brought her out of her shell and I don't want this to set her back."

Everyone was busy with Christmas preparations. In addition to the normal gift buying and food shopping, there was to be a carol concert at school the evening before the last day of term. A number of the teachers were involved in rehearsals for it, and parents were committed to running their offspring to and from those. As a result, volunteer, interest in the theatre was waning even further. One night only Grace, Sean, Lizzie and Ed turned up.

"Oh, this doesn't look good." Ed looked crestfallen, no doubt imaging his pet project was about to grind to a halt.

"They'll come back." Lizzie stood on tiptoes so she could offer a reassuring kiss on his cheek. "Once Christmas is over and Montcraig reverts to its usual sleepy self they'll be keen to have something to do in the evenings."

"In the meantime," Grace added, "the four of us should do as much as we can, because there will be times in the next few weeks when even we'll be too busy to make it."

She and Sean made their way up to the old office. It was becoming a familiar journey now and Grace was no longer worried about the rickety old staircase that ascended into darkness. But Sean still took her hand as he'd done every other time since that first one, and she was happy to let him.

"You're cold," he said as his fingers folded around hers.

"I lost my gloves."

Once they got to the office he rubbed her hands with his and she was grateful for the heat that warmed her fingers.

"Sean," she said in surprise. "What are you doing?"

"You won't be able to work efficiently if you're frozen." He smiled in response.

The office was unrecognisable from when they'd first arrived. They'd worked hard and, even though a number of papers still waited to be sorted, most had been taken in black refuse sacks to the recycling centre.

"It's actually a really nice room," Grace said, looking around the large area they'd cleared. It was plain by comparison to the rest of the theatre, which made perfect sense, as it was unlikely visitors would have come up here, but it was large, with huge windows that overlooked Montcraig. Once they were cleaned there would be lots of natural daylight.

"It would make a great artist studio," Sean said thoughtfully.

Grace knew he was right.

"Lizzie mentioned she thinks Ed's planning to rent out some of the space," she suggested gently. "Perhaps you could see if it might be possible for you to have this as your own studio."

She saw an interested gleam in his blue eyes for a moment and she knew he'd liked the suggestion.

"I can imagine you up here away from the world, with your paints and your canvases." She looked around, picturing the scene. He'd be wearing his paint-splattered jeans, a look of intense concentration on his face. "You deserve a decent studio. It must be impossible to work freely in the cottage."

She'd seen some of his work and he was good. Easily good enough to justify renting out his own studio. Then she frowned, because someone that talented would have been creating art all their lives, and she hadn't known that about him until he'd returned as a teacher. She mustn't have known him very well at all in those days.

"Any news on the collection?" she asked as she shuffled through the ever-dwindling bundle of papers. The question was more to distract herself from the worrying train of thought about the past rather than anything else.

"Ed heard back from the solicitors and everything in the building was included in the sale."

"That's good news."

"It is. They also went out to speak to Jim Aitken."

"The reclusive farmer who lives at the edge of town?"

Sean nodded.

"There's a story about him." Grace frowned, trying to remember. "I don't know him. He's never been around town much that I can remember. But I do recall my mother saying something about a broken love affair. He moved out to that farm when his sweetheart moved away and became a bit of a recluse."

"He worked here in the box office when he was younger. He said it was the owners who gave instructions to keep all this stuff. They were proud of their theatre and wanted a record of all the performances. It became a tradition that was carried on over the years."

She liked the idea. She hoped the committee would decide to carry on the tradition. She would push for them to.

"So we won't be treading on any toes if we do make copies of the photographs and sell the duplicate programmes?"

Sean shook his head.

"No, it all belongs to the theatre. Ed's asked me to go through and see what we can sell, then organise a permanent display for when we've finished renovating."

"That sounds like a lot of work on top of what you're already doing with the drama group and in the theatre."

"I don't mind." Sean smiled. "It's not as though I have anything else to do with my spare time."

That hit home and she realised how unfair she'd been. He was freshly back in town; most of the friends he'd known as he was growing up had left. And the one who hadn't – Grace herself – was busy keeping him at arm's length. What kind of friend would do that?

A bad one, that was what. She'd always prided herself on being there for the people she cared about. And she had cared about Sean once – still did, to a certain extent.

"How about next time we have an evening off from here we do something?" she suggested.

He glanced over uncertainly.

"Are you asking me out on a date, Grace Anderson?"

She felt her cheeks blush.

"Not a date. Just spend some time together. Maybe go to the cinema or something. As friends."

"That would be nice."

He stared at her for a moment, making her feel she maybe shouldn't have said anything. But when she put herself in his position, she knew she'd done the right thing. He had made new friends amongst the other teachers, but they were all busy at this time of year with their families and preparing for Christmas productions.

She gave a little shrug.

"We single teachers have to stick together."

He laughed.

"There are fewer of us than ever in Montcraig these days."

"You heard about Lizzie and Ed?"

"He told me. He seemed stunned by the development."

"Lizzie doesn't hang around once she decides something. He won't have known what hit him."

"He seemed stunned but pleased," Sean amended.

She smiled as she put a pile of old papers into a bin bag.

"He's loved her for a long time. Of course he's pleased."

For some reason she glanced over and the look in his eyes made her pause. They made a connection across the room and she was mesmerised by the force of it.

"Sean . . . I . . ." She forced herself to look away and when she glanced back the moment was gone.

"It's getting late. We should finish up here for tonight. Why don't you come back to my place? You can see my ideas for displaying the collection and maybe share a pizza?"

She thought for a moment. She really wanted to see what was happening with the old photos and programmes they'd unearthed. She really couldn't face going home to cook a lonely supper if there was an alternative. Besides, she found she wanted to spend more time with Sean, which wasn't surprising as he was very good company.

"Yes, please, I'd like that."

Her reward was a grin of megawatt proportions that made her tingle all the way down to her toes.

"Come on, then, let's go." He held out his hand, and, instead of taking it, she walked closer and leaned against him. Then she rested her head against his chest for just a second and allowed him to bring his arms around her and hold her tight.

She didn't know why she did it. But it seemed the right thing to do.

Those brief moments, holding Grace in his arms,

reminded Sean of how life could have been. If he hadn't left her. If she had gone with him. Might they be married by now? Maybe they would have had children by now.

But Sean didn't often allow himself the luxury of dreaming. He'd long since forced himself to be a realist, and the reality was that he had left and Grace had stayed.

They were both still young, though. There was time to make good the mistakes of the past. Maybe.

He needed to take things slowly. Their relationship still had some distance to go. But when he thought of his first day back in Montcraig, when she'd stepped into oncoming traffic rather than face him, he knew they were moving in the right direction.

She'd just accepted an invitation to share a late supper with him, then she'd stepped into his arms for a hug.

"Sean?" Grace's tone was concerned and her steps faltered as they rounded the corner to his house. "There's someone at your door."

That was odd. It was dark and it was late.

"Who'd be visiting at this time?"

"It looks like Jim Aitken," she added as they neared.

Sean frowned as they approached.

"Is there something wrong?" he asked the man.

Jim shook his head.

"No, nothing wrong. And I'm sorry to bother you at this time of night," he told them. "But once I made up my mind I couldn't wait."

"Made up your mind about what?" Sean asked.

"It's the photographs," he said. "The ones from the theatre. They say you have them here. I wonder if I could trouble you for a look at them, please."

Even though Sean was desperate to spend time alone with Grace, there was no way he could send the older man away.

"Why don't you come in?" he invited.

# Second Chances

GRACE could see Jim's hands were trembling as he sat at Sean's table and looked through the memorabilia. Eventually he stopped flicking through the photographs and picked one up.

It was a photo of a young woman that had caught his attention.

"Who was that?" she asked gently.

Jim smiled but didn't take his eyes off the photo.

"That was Daisy."

Grace recalled what she knew of the story she'd told Sean the other night and suddenly she understood. This was his lost love; the woman who had caused him to retreat from life and move out of town to live on his own.

"Do you want to talk about her?" she asked.

Jim looked up, and there was such a sad look in his pale blue eyes that Grace held her breath. Then he began to talk.

"There's not much to tell, really, lass. Daisy came with a group of travelling actors. They were here for a few weeks and we saw a lot of each other. Fell in love. Then she left. Had to go with the troupe, you see."

"Did you ask her to stay?" Sean asked.

"Aye, I did. And she asked me to go with her, but neither of us was prepared to give in."

Grace caught Sean's eye and felt incredibly sad. Jim might have been talking about her and Sean. But Sean had done what Daisy hadn't – he'd come back.

"I can make copies of these photographs for you," Sean said. "I'm sure the committee won't have any objection."

"Thank you, lad." Jim's smile held a world of sadness. "I don't know if I've left it too late, but seeing these photos have made my mind up. I'm going to try to find Daisy. See what became of her. Make sure she's happy, if nothing else."

It was late by the time Jim left. Grace got to her feet.

"I should go, too."

"We haven't had our pizza yet."

"Yes, but . . ."

"It's Friday night," he coaxed. "You can have a lie-in tomorrow morning."

Her tummy rumbled loudly and they both laughed.

"Seems my digestive system agrees with you."

They sat in the living-room to eat. Grace looked around at the changes since she was last here.

"I like what you've done with this room."

The walls were now a warm red and he'd polished the floorboards. Lamps dotted around the room added soft lighting and the soft furnishings in cream complemented the colour scheme.

He grinned.

"Glad you like it. It's not finished yet, though. I still have to get some paintings for the walls."

"Ones you've painted yourself?"

"Some."

They lapsed into an easy silence while they finished their meal and then both began to speak at once, then both stopped to allow the other to have their say.

Grace giggled nervously in the silence.

"You go first," he urged.

Grace nodded.

"Jim's story was so sad."

"So many wasted years," Sean agreed.

"We shouldn't let that happen to us."

He sat back and his eyes narrowed as he looked at her.

"What are you suggesting, Grace?"

"Well, maybe . . ." She cleared her throat and looked at the floor. Suddenly it was very difficult to speak and her heart was beating so rapidly she thought she might pass out.

She took a deep breath, lifted her eyes to meet his confused expression and tried again. "Maybe it's not too late for us to try again."

All the colour left Sean's face and he got to his feet.

"Do you mean that, Grace?"

She nodded.

"I never say things I don't mean. I haven't changed in that respect."

He stood uncertainly and then stepped towards her, holding out his hand.

She smiled and reached out to him. When their fingers met she knew she'd made the right decision. This time she wasn't stressed or worried – the only emotion she felt was happiness.

His hand curled around hers and he pulled her to her feet. She looked up into burning blue eyes.

"I never thought I'd hear you say that. I'd hoped, but you seemed so dead set against our relationship being anything other than platonic."

"I was."

"So what changed your mind?"

She smiled up at him, lifted her free hand and stroked his face.

"You're still Sean McIver. I'm still susceptible to your charm."

He laughed.

"I've been trying to use my charm to convince you to go out with me since I got back."

How did she explain? She'd started to believe he'd changed when he'd coped so capably with their runaway teens on the trip, and his treatment of Jim tonight had cemented her opinion – Sean McIver had grown up.

"OK, it's lots of things. But then seeing Jim tonight, hearing his story – well, it's all so sad. All those wasted years missing Daisy when they could have been together."

He pulled her closer and kissed her lightly on the lips and she felt that kiss all the way down to her toes. Yes, the old magic was still there. She looked up into his eyes, his arms still around her.

"So, this cinema outing you were talking about . . . Why don't we speak to Ed and suggest we take the day off from working on the theatre tomorrow? We can have a meal, too."

She nodded.

"That can be our first proper date."

"Well, not exactly our first date." He reminded her. "I know it was a long time ago, but our relationship did mean a lot to me, you know."

Warmth spread through her and she lifted her arms around his neck.

"To me, too. That's why I was scared of letting myself fall for you again. I still am, if I'm honest."

He frowned.

"Well, if it makes you feel a bit easier about things, we could take every day as it comes. No pressure and no expectations. Just two friends who like each other and enjoy each other's company spending time together, and seeing where things lead."

It seemed he understood her exactly, which proved she was right to give him another chance.

"I think I like the sound of that, Sean McIver."

His dark head swooped and he dropped another kiss on her mouth.

"It's really late now. I'll walk you home, or we'll both be too tired to watch any film tomorrow."

\*　　　　\*　　　　\*　　　　\*

Sean's head buzzed with this new development as he made his way home after dropping Grace at her door. He had begun to doubt the wisdom of coming back to

Montcraig after so many years. He'd worried that taking a job just because Grace worked at the same school was asking for trouble. But, after tonight, it seemed his fears were ungrounded.

OK, she hadn't declared undying love, but the fact Grace was prepared to give their relationship another go meant the world to him. He hadn't been able to get her out of his mind in all the years he'd been away.

And he'd tried. When she'd refused to go travelling as they'd planned, he'd been hurt and he'd run off to lick his wounds. By the time he'd realised she'd had every right to take up her university place, it had been too late.

He phoned Ed first thing in the morning.

"I think that's a good idea," Ed replied to the suggestion. "If the other volunteers think they can wind down for the Christmas break, then we should be able to as well."

"There was just one other thing." Quickly Sean explained about his late-night visitor the night before. "So I was wondering if it would be acceptable to copy some of the photos for Jim. Just the ones of Daisy."

"I think that's an excellent idea. We want to keep the originals in the theatre for everyone to enjoy, but the least we can do is let the man have copies."

With that sorted, Sean looked online for film times in the multi-screen theatre in the neighbouring town, then he booked a table at the nicest restaurant he knew. He phoned Grace.

"Hello, Grace Anderson speaking." She sounded sleepy and he smiled, imagining her hair a riot of blonde tangled curls around her lovely face.

"Hey, sleepyhead. Did I wake you?"

"Yes."

He could hear the hint of a smile in her voice and it sent his spine tingling.

"I'm sorry."

"It's OK. I should have been up ages ago."

He explained that he'd spoken to Ed and checked his choice of film was to her taste.

"Oh, I really wanted to see that!" She was so animated he knew she wasn't just being polite. "I didn't think I'd have time, though, and thought I'd have to wait for it to come out on DVD."

"Nothing like going to the pictures for . . . well, I suppose an authentic cinema experience." He knew he was talking gibberish, but he couldn't help it. He was quite keen to keep her on the phone for a while – even if he was going to see her soon.

She wasn't having any of it.

"Sean, I'd better go. I have to go for a shower and I've some marking to do before we can go out to play."

"OK, Grace. I'll see you later."

Having been excused from his duties at the theatre, Sean set about sorting through the photographs. It took him a good few hours to scan in and print off copies of the ones Jim had shown an interest in.

The last one was a photo of Jim and Daisy together. Really, if these belonged to him, he'd let Jim have the original. But they didn't, so he dutifully scanned it in.

He managed to enlarge it and it printed beautifully.

He found a frame and popped it in. No doubt it would make Jim sad to see it, but he also knew that the past few years he would have been very grateful for any reminder of Grace.

"We need to stop off at Jim's on the way," he told Grace later. "I've copied those photos for him."

Grace stayed in the car – there wasn't long until their film started, so this was just a flying visit.

"He told us to pop by if we're passing," he told Grace.

Her eyes widened in surprise.

"But he doesn't like visitors."

Sean laughed.

"Seems he's changing his mind."

They enjoyed the film. Although it was more of a chick flick than his usual tastes would have run to, the company more than made up for it.

There was a bit of a commotion as they left the cinema after the film had finished. A group of boys were behaving boisterously in the foyer.

"Don't we know those boys?" he asked Grace.

"Unfortunately. It's Callum and the rowdier members of his collection of friends."

He toyed with the idea of going over and telling them to keep the noise down, but one of the cinema workers intervened before he could do anything.

The noisy party were very nearly out of the door when they spotted Sean and Grace.

"Hey, Miss Anderson!" Callum shouted as he pointed at Sean. "Are you sure he's not your boyfriend."

Grace treated the boy to a look that silenced him at 50 paces.

Sean was impressed. She seemed so gentle and quiet, but she'd mastered the kind of glance most teachers would pay good money to be able to perfect.

"That told him." He laughed as they headed out to the car.

Grace giggled.

"Let's go for that meal, I'm starving."

She couldn't hide her surprise when she saw where they were going to eat.

"If I'd known we were coming here I'd have made a bit more effort with my appearance."

He glanced at her. She was wearing trousers and a top – her ordinary clothes, but with her face and figure she could have been wearing a potato sack and she'd still have been beautiful.

"You look fine to me."

A soft blush warmed her face and his protective instinct went into overdrive.

*        *        *        *

Sean was doing and saying all the right things and it all seemed entirely natural rather than an act put on for her benefit.

It had started with his copying those photos so quickly for Jim. It must have taken him hours and Grace was immediately impressed that he'd gone to so much trouble for someone he hardly knew. Even the choice of film had obviously been made with her in mind.

"This food is just heavenly," she told him as she reached over and offered a forkful of seafood lasagne. "Try this."

He leaned across the table and took her hand to guide the fork into his mouth. Grace's breath caught. It was all unbearably intimate – the kind of gesture a girlfriend might make and a boyfriend might accept.

This was quickly becoming a reality. Seemed she was going to have to get used to the kind of encounter they'd had with Callum and his friends earlier. Since Sean had come back, the whole town had been holding their breath to see if Grace would be won over by his charm a second time.

She glanced across the table. She very much thought Sean might well be worth putting up with being the object of talk.

# Christmas Time

I CAN'T believe it!" Lizzie scowled as she got up to rinse her cup in the staff room sink. "You and Sean McIver. After everything you said when he first came back." Her bangles jingled as she ran her fingers through her hair.

"A girl's allowed to change her mind."

"I know, but Sean McIver! What if he takes off again?"

Grace knew Lizzie was speaking out of concern for her, so she tried not to get too annoyed.

"We're just taking things slowly at the moment. Nobody has made any promises and nobody has any expectations."

There was a flurry of activity as they were joined by colleagues, all in a happy mood because of the holiday.

"Just be careful, Grace," Lizzie said quietly so only Grace could hear. "I don't want him hurting you again."

Grace nodded. Part of her was pleased she had a friend like Lizzie to look out for her, and the rest slightly miffed she was so negative about Sean.

The afternoon passed quickly.

"I'll see you at church on Christmas Eve," Lizzie said as she gave Grace a hug.

Grace hugged her back.

"The cake's all ready for the big day. The mince-pies, too. Is there anything else I can bring?"

Lizzie shook her head.

"Just yourself."

"It will be odd without Mum and Dad. It's the first Christmas I've ever spent without them. I'm so glad I have you as a friend."

Lizzie raised an eyebrow.

"I'm sure you're pleased now that I thought to invite Sean."

Grace smiled. Of course she was pleased. Even if they

weren't taking tentative steps to repair their relationship, she'd still have been pleased because she'd have hated him to be on his own.

"What time do you want me to get there?"

"Any time as long as it's before midday. Ed's helping me with lunch so I won't need you to muck in."

The next few days passed quickly. Grace had always been a last-minute Christmas shopper and this year was no exception. She rushed around until she was practically dizzy, being jostled by crowds and loving every minute.

She did wonder if she should be better organised. She was a Maths teacher, after all, and she liked things neat and ordered. But whizzing around the shops in the few days before Christmas had always been part of the season for her.

\*　　　\*　　　\*　　　\*

Grace was the last to arrive at Lizzie's house on Christmas morning. It looked as though Ed had been there since daybreak, as he was well settled into the kitchen. Sean was setting the table.

Grace felt slightly guilty that she was doing too little and she rushed to help with the cutlery and the napkins.

"Merry Christmas!" Sean greeted her from the other side of the table.

She looked up and her tummy flipped as he smiled. For a minute she couldn't do anything but stare at him. Then Lizzie and Ed started to bring through the serving dishes.

"Your parents are still away?" Ed asked as the vegetables were passed around the Christmas table for everyone to help themselves.

"Yes. It's a six-month cruise. They haven't had a holiday in years," Grace explained. "So they decided they might as well make it a good one." And, she didn't add, they both deserved a break after everything they'd been through.

"When are they back?" Sean asked.

"Not for a while," Grace smiled sadly. She missed them both so much. "Mum wasn't keen to stay away from Montcraig, especially not at New Year. She didn't want to miss the party, but Dad persuaded her."

"It's not like them, though," Lizzie added. "Staying away so long. You're mum's a homebody. Like you."

She was aware of Sean's eyes on her. Was he thinking of just how much of a homebody Grace herself had been, all those years ago?

"She just never had the chance before. From what I've heard back they're both having a wonderful time."

Her parents had phoned her this morning and it had been lovely to speak to them again. She couldn't wait for them to arrive home. But when her mother had asked for any news, Grace had been very careful with what she'd passed on. She'd happily told her mother about the school trip, about the theatre and even about Jim Aitken, but she had painstakingly edited out any reference of Sean.

She didn't know how her mother would react, and she didn't want to spoil what was left of their holiday. There would be plenty of time to tell them when they arrived home. If she told them face to face, there would be less chance for upset. It was all a matter of finding the right time.

"This is delicious, Lizzie." Sean broke into the silence.

"It is," Grace agreed, glad for the opportunity to think of something less worrying. "I'd like to say that I'll make Christmas dinner for the four of us next year, but I know it would barely be edible."

Everyone laughed. They all knew Grace tried, but her attempts at cooking were legendary for all the wrong reasons.

"I can cook Christmas lunch next year," Sean offered.

Three surprised faces looked his way.

"You can cook?" Lizzie asked in surprise.

"Of course I can. Why are you so shocked?"

Grace saw Lizzie take in Sean's appearance.

"You don't look like you can cook. You look like you should be gracing the pages of a magazine as a male model."

There was a moment of silence then Grace giggled.

"Just because Sean's good-looking doesn't mean he's useless in the kitchen."

"You weren't surprised when I helped you make dinner," Ed broke in and they all laughed. Ed wasn't bad-looking, but they all knew it was unlikely a photographer would be after him for a fashion shoot in the near future, because he didn't have Sean's air of confidence and self-assurance.

There was a moment when Ed looked a little crestfallen, but then his lips twitched and soon he was laughing as loudly as everyone else.

"So you're still planning to be around next year, Sean?" There didn't seem to be any nastiness about Lizzie's question, but Grace still gasped.

She didn't want to hear Sean's reply but, short of putting her fingers in her ears, she had no choice but to listen.

Sean glanced at Grace.

"I've no plans to go anywhere."

"Good," Ed chipped in. "Because Lizzie and I have a favour to ask the two of you."

"We're getting married!" Lizzie chimed in with a shriek. "Can you believe it? All this time he was under my nose and I just didn't realise."

Grace and Sean got to their feet. There was much hugging and smiling and hand-shaking, then they resumed their meal.

"So," Grace asked when it seemed the start of this conversation had been forgotten. "What's this favour?"

"We're having a small wedding," Lizzie explained. "Just a minister, the two of us and two witnesses."

"We wondered," Ed said, "if you would be our witnesses?"

There was more hugging and smiling and hand-shaking.

"Do I take it that's a yes?" Lizzie laughed as they all settled down again.

"Of course!" Grace grinned. "Have you set a date?"

Lizzie and Ed glanced at each other again.

"The first day of the February break," he said.

"That quickly?" Grace was surprised. She had expected they would have months of looking forward to the wedding.

"No point hanging around," Ed reasoned. "Lizzie didn't want a big wedding so it didn't take long to arrange."

Grace looked at Lizzie as she realised what a small wedding would mean.

"But don't you want people there? Colleagues? Other friends? Family?" She knew Lizzie and Ed didn't have much family, but each had distant cousins.

"I've done the big wedding thing," Lizzie reminded her softly. "And it didn't work out. So this time I thought I'd try small and hopefully I'll get my happy ever after."

Grace reached out and covered her friend's hand with her own.

"I'm sure this time that's exactly what you'll get."

It was late by the time Sean and Grace decided to go. With all the talk of weddings at Lizzie's house, Sean was at a bit of a loss as to what to say to Grace on the walk home. Their renewed relationship was very much in its early stages, but he'd wanted to marry her once. Very much. In fact, he'd never been able to imagine marrying anyone else.

She slipped her gloved hand in his and her pace slowed a little as she glanced up at the clear night sky. The stars were bright and there was a bite in the air.

"You're very quiet," she said at last.

Even though he knew it was a bad idea, he found he couldn't stop himself from mentioning it.

"What kind of wedding would you want?"

He knew he'd made a mistake when he saw the expression that crossed her face. This wasn't mild discomfort – it was pure horror.

"That wasn't a proposal," he rushed to reassure her.

Grace stopped walking and he could read the expression on her face in the yellow sodium light from the streetlamp above them. She still wasn't happy.

"I was wondering, that was all. Just with all the talk of weddings . . ." He shut up.

He could feel the already frozen night become even chillier as she continued to stare at him.

"I know," she said at last through unsmiling lips. "It just seemed odd to have you ask me that question."

"Don't you want to get married one day?"

"One day, perhaps. But not yet."

He watched as she bit her even white teeth into her lip.

Ah, well, he could handle that. It wasn't as though he was in any hurry to get married himself. They were both still young, after all. And look how far their relationship had progressed already. Maybe, by the time he was ready to propose, she'd be of a mind to accept.

With a sigh, he gathered her close.

"No pressure, Grace," he told her as he rested his face on the top of her head and breathed in the clean scent of her shampoo. "We agreed."

He felt her nod and then she sighed.

"I'm sorry, Sean. You spooked me with that question."

He felt her relax in his arms and he longed for the uncomplicated company they'd shared only a few minutes ago. Why had he opened his big mouth?

"It's cold," he said. "Let's hurry before we both freeze."

As they arrived back at her flat, it was beginning to snow.

"A magical end to the day," she commented as she unlocked the door, but her tone was flat. "Do you want to come in for a cup of tea?"

It was late, but he wasn't ready to leave her yet.

"Yes, thank you."

"There's still a party at the Montcraig Hotel at Hogmanay," she explained as she found the tea pot and put the kettle on.

"I remember going to the New Year parties as a teenager," he told her.

Then she smiled and he knew everything between them was all right.

He drank the tea she'd made for him with quiet contentment. But, as she took his empty cup, there was frantic knocking at the door.

"Who's that?" she asked, startled. "Nobody ever calls by at this time of night." Her face was pale and she made no move to answer the door.

The knocking came again and Sean got to his feet.

"I'll see who it is. It sounds like it might be urgent."

He recognised Grace's neighbour, Mrs McDonald. She looked frantic with worry.

"Thank goodness," she cried as she grabbed his arm and pulled him towards the open door to her flat. "I need help. My husband's choking and he can't breathe."

Sean had done some first aid and knew the basics.

He followed Mrs McDonald into the flat next door.

"Have you phoned for an ambulance?" he asked the woman as he approached her choking husband.

"It's on its way. Do something, please!" the distraught woman cried.

Sean used the heel of his hand and administered a few firm slaps to the man's upper back.

Nothing happened.

"Please," Mrs McDonald said again. "He's turning blue."

Doing his best to keep calm, Sean tried another five firm back slaps. He heaved a sigh of relief when there was coughing and spluttering as the blockage was dislodged and Reg McDonald started to breathe again.

"What's going on?" Grace asked from the door.

"Your young man is a hero," Mrs McDonald declared, going over to Sean and enveloping him in a tight hug. "He's a lifesaver."

"I don't understand." Grace blinked, her confusion unmistakeable.

"We were eating turkey sandwiches," Mrs McDonald told her. "Reg complained the meat was a bit dry, and the next thing I knew he was choking and turning blue."

"Oh, no. How awful!"

"I panicked. I heard you come in a short while ago so I hoped you'd still be awake."

"I would have been happy to help if I could," Grace confirmed. "But I don't have any medical training."

"Well, thank goodness Sean was there," Mrs McDonald remarked and gave him another hug. "Are you all right now, dear?" she asked her husband.

A red-faced Reg McDonald nodded.

"Hopefully the ambulance will be here soon," Sean told them. "I know basic first aid, but Reg should probably be checked out. You've both had quite a fright."

The paramedics arrived within minutes so Sean and Grace left them to it.

Of course, they needed another cup of tea to calm down after all the excitement.

"I'm impressed," Grace told him.

"You'd have done the same," he assured her.

"Perhaps." She smiled. "I don't know if I'd have been successful. Hopefully we'll never have the chance to find out. A brush with death like that is upsetting for everyone."

"It was nothing," he dismissed, embarrassed. He'd done no more than anyone else would have done.

"So, tell me. How did you know what to do?"

He told her about the first aid courses he'd been on and about the man in a restaurant in Thailand who'd been choking and had had luckily been saved by a doctor who'd been dining at the same place.

"So you'd seen the procedure performed once and knew what to do."

"I had no choice but to try," he told her. "Reg wouldn't have survived if we'd had to wait for the paramedics."

"Just as well you were here," she said, reaching for his hand.

The feel of her warm fingers wrapped around his made him feel he really was a hero.

\*         \*         \*         \*

Sean called for Grace on Boxing Day. He was warmly wrapped up in walking gear.

"Look at you, all dressed for an expedition," she teased.

"I've come to take you out."

"I meant to have a quiet day," she told him with a laugh. "Especially as we had such a late night last night."

"I wanted to see you," he said.

As she looked into his electric blue eyes, she knew she had wanted to see him, too. It was just that she hadn't realised until this moment.

"I've packed a picnic."

"A picnic?" She was aghast as she glanced out of the window at the dusting of snow that now covered their world. "It's freezing."

"We can eat in the car. I thought it would be good to get out of Montcraig for a couple of hours and walk."

She nodded. She liked the sound of that.

"I'll get my walking gear."

She quickly found her warmest clothes: fleece, hat, gloves and walking boots. Then she joined him.

"Now I'm dressed for an expedition, too!"

He drove them out of town.

"There's a lot I don't know about you," she told him. "I

realised last night you've lived a whole different life in the time you were away."

"I suppose I did, in a way. But I only travelled for a year."

"You obviously did a lot in that year." A lot of things that separated the people they were now from their shared past.

"It's not too late for you to travel, Grace. We could even plan a trip together. In the summer holidays, perhaps."

"Perhaps." She couldn't give him a definite answer – not yet. Not when she didn't know how things would work out between them. The summer seemed a long way away from where they were in the middle of winter.

The roads were clear of snow and had been gritted, so they made good progress. Soon they arrived at a car park a short way out of town.

"How do you feel about walking to the summit?" Sean waved at the sharp incline in front of them.

She took a deep breath. It wasn't her idea of a relaxing day, but how could she refuse when he'd gone to so much trouble?

"Love to." She reached out her hand and let him guide her towards the path that would take them to the top.

It was a beautiful day; crisp and bright with clear blue skies. The view from the summit over Montcraig was breathtaking.

"Worth the effort?" Sean asked.

She looked up into his handsome face and smiled.

"Definitely."

He slipped his arms around her waist and pulled her closer so he could plant a kiss on the end of her nose.

"You're cold."

She looked around at the snow. It was still only a dusting, but clear proof of how low the temperature was.

"And you're surprised?"

"Maybe this was a daft idea."

She shook her head.

"No. It was a lovely idea."

"We probably shouldn't linger too long. The temperature's set to drop later this afternoon and they've promised more snow."

She looked incredulously up at the clear sky.

"Are you sure? They have been known to be wrong."

"The weather can turn in a moment, and we'd best not risk it."

Their descent was much quicker, but by the time they reached the car the sky had turned grey.

"Looks like you were right," she said as fat snowflakes fell around them.

They hurried into the shelter of the car.

"I'd thought we could eat lunch here," he said. "But that snow seems very heavy, so it might be as well to take our picnic back to my place before the roads get too bad."

She could see his warm breath condense in the air as he spoke and she nodded in agreement.

"Your place is probably the best idea."

"I didn't think it would hit us this early."

She liked that he'd planned this for them. Maybe a walk up a frozen hill wouldn't have been her choice of a Boxing Day activity, but she'd really enjoyed herself.

"Today's been fun," she told him as they reached the outskirts of Montcraig.

He laughed and the sound cheered her up.

"I suspect you're being kind."

"Not at all."

"In any case, you can choose our next outing."

She smiled, knowing she'd enjoy being anywhere as long as he was there. She might not be ready to marry him, but there was no denying he was good company.

"New Year's Eve," she suggested with a grin. "Want to take me to the party at the Montcraig Hotel?"

## Happy New Year

SEAN held Grace's hand in a tight grip as they walked. The road was icy and her high-heeled shoes entirely unsuitable for the sharp incline. And, although she seemed sure-footed, he wanted to be ready if she did slip.

He glanced at her. She was looking stunning tonight in a simple midnight blue dress that left her arms and one shoulder bare. She'd thrown a coat over her shoulders for the walk to the party.

"Are you cold?"

She shook her head.

Neither was he, which was surprising because their breath was visible in the crisp night air. They were making their way to where the hotel stood, lit up like a beacon, on the hill overlooking town. They and the rest of the population of Montcraig, it seemed.

In the years since he'd last been to the Hogmanay party, it seemed the event had grown.

"I don't remember so many people going to the party before."

"You've forgotten." She laughed. "It was always standing room only. It's a popular event."

"Come on, let's hurry." The temperature had fallen way below zero and her dress wasn't made of the kind of material that would have made lingering outdoors fun for her.

They climbed up the steps at the front of the building and Sean opened the door.

It was the heat that hit him first, then the noise.

"Hey, you two!" a female voice shouted from nearby. "Over here."

He turned to find Lizzie waving wildly and pointing to the far corner.

"We've got a table. Ed and Harriet are guarding it. I'm just going to fetch drinks."

He allowed Grace to pull him towards the table where their friends sat and Lizzie arrived a moment later with a laden tray.

"That was quick," Grace told her.

"I charmed my way to the front of the queue." She grinned.

"You pushed in?"

Lizzie laughed at Grace's outrage.

"Of course not, but there was a line of parents from the school ahead and they waved me on. One of the perks of being a teacher."

"That's never happened to me," Grace said.

"Nor me," Ed agreed as Harriet nodded in agreement.

They'd only been seated five minutes when Jim Aiken came up to the table.

"I thought you'd want to know about my search for Daisy," he told them, his face unsmiling.

"Have you found her?" Grace asked gently.

Jim nodded.

"Well, not her, exactly. I found her family. She married shortly after she left Montcraig. He was another actor in the company and they had two children. She was widowed in her forties."

"Where is she now?" Grace asked softly.

Jim shook his head.

Grace gasped and got to her feet.

"You mean . . .?"

"I was too late. She died last year."

Grace gave him a tentative hug.

"Why don't you join us?"

"Yes." Sean got to his feet and went to pull another chair up to the table. "Please do."

"It's very kind of you to ask, but I'm trying to renew

acquaintances tonight." Jim sighed. "Trying to rebuild my life. I'm sad about Daisy, of course, but she got on with her life after leaving here."

While he hadn't, Sean realised. Jim had lived in a state of almost suspended animation – waiting, broken-hearted, for his lost love. Sean guessed, if the rumours were true, this was the first time Jim had been in town for any kind of party in decades.

"Sit with us for a moment," he urged. "Let me get you a drink."

Jim gave a brief nod and Sean headed for the bar.

Considering how busy it was, it took him no time to be served. The hotel was well staffed by efficient workers. He realised as he saw the queue moving that everyone got preferential treatment here – not only teachers, as Lizzie led them to believe.

As he made his way back, Sean gave silent thanks for his good sense in coming back for Grace before four decades had passed by. He suppressed a shudder as he realised that even eight years might have been too long, if she'd met someone else.

Jim didn't stay with them long. The ceilidh band was setting up and he was eager to get back to his own renewed friendships.

As they watched Jim walk away, Grace leaned in towards Sean and he breathed in her familiar scent.

"So sad," she muttered into his ear.

He could only nod in agreement.

As the music started, Sean could feel Grace move at his side in time to the music and he forced down his feelings of sadness at the ending to Jim and Daisy's story and he smiled. Grace had always loved to dance. He got to his feet.

"How about it?" He held his hand and looked at her expectantly.

She hesitated for a moment and he thought she might

refuse, but then she smiled.

"I hadn't been planning to dance. But why not?" She kicked her unsuitable shoes off and took his hand.

They did two rounds of the Gay Gordons and then Lizzie joined them for the Dashing White Sergeant.

Grace was breathless by the time they took their seats again, her soft cheeks red with the effort and the fun of dancing.

"The band's good," Sean commented. "Do you remember the crackly old records we used to dance to?"

She laughed.

"Yes. But everyone always enjoyed themselves, despite the lack of decent live music."

"But there's no comparison to what the event has obviously grown into."

"We've learned how to celebrate in Montcraig." She laughed. "Wait here and I'll go and fetch some drinks to help us cool down."

Confirming his opinion on the efficiency of the hotel's staff, she was back before he knew it.

"It's years since I've been to a ceilidh. I didn't think I'd remember how to do those dances," he confided as he took a tall drink of lemonade and orange juice from her.

"You never forget," she replied. "Not when they get you young by making you learn at school."

He felt himself smiling as he remembered the gym lessons in the run up to Christmas every year, when the whole school had been forced to dance. It had been excruciating for the self-conscious teenagers. He'd hated every minute until Grace had shyly approached him during a girls' choice.

That had been the first time he'd danced with Grace and he'd made sure he'd danced every dance with her after that.

Just as he intended to do tonight.

She was equally eager. He'd hardly caught his breath

before she was pulling him on to his feet again.

"OK." He laughed. "Take it easy!"

"I'd forgotten how much fun this is. It's a while since I've danced."

He felt that stab at his heart. He hoped it wasn't his fault she hadn't danced in a while.

"When did you last dance, Grace?"

She smiled sadly up at him.

"The last time you took me to the New Year's Eve Party."

"But why? You've been out with other men."

"None of them were particularly light on their feet. I never went out with any of them long enough to bother teaching them."

Although he was still worried she hadn't danced since he'd left, knowing that, in some ways, he was irreplaceable in Grace's life made Sean feel better.

By the time they arrived back at the table for the second time, one of Grace's shoes had disappeared.

Sean helped her look, but it was nowhere to be seen.

"Someone will have kicked it under another table," Harriet assured them. "We'll find it, I'm sure."

But, despite involving the surrounding tables in the search, the shoe wasn't found.

"I feel like Cinderella," she said. "I'll have to walk home barefoot."

"You can't do that," Lizzie said. "It's freezing out there. Plus you might injure yourself by stepping on something in the dark."

"So how do you suggest I get home?" Grace asked. "If I don't walk home without shoes I'll have to stay here all night. I'm guessing I won't be able to get a taxi tonight."

"I'll carry you," Sean offered. It would be no problem; she barely weighed anything in any case.

"Ah," the women around the table said in unison.

"That's so romantic," Lizzie added with a grin.

Grace was smiling, but shaking her head.

"I can't let you do that. I'll give you a hernia."

"No, you won't." He leaned forward so only she could hear his next words. "When I lifted you out of the path of Harriet's car your weight barely registered." He didn't add that the impression those brief moments had made on his mind had regularly kept him awake as he recalled the scent of her hair and the warmth of her body in his arms.

"But it's quite a walk back."

"I'll give you a piggy back."

She giggled and pushed the blonde curls out of her eyes.

"Seriously, Sean? You think it's a good idea for a teacher to give another teacher a piggy back through the streets of Montcraig in the dead of night?"

"It's a better idea than one of those teachers hurting herself by trying to walk home with no shoes on in the middle of winter."

"Well . . . OK, then," she finally agreed, though she didn't look too sure about it.

Everyone was counting down to the bells now and, short of arguing into the New Year, she'd obviously decided it was best just to go along with his suggestion.

\*　　　\*　　　\*　　　\*

With handbag slung over her shoulder and her one remaining shoe in one hand, Grace stepped off her chair in stockinged feet and climbed on to Sean's back. As she wound her arms firmly around his neck, she knew she was asking for trouble. Not only was she enjoying being so close to him a little more than she ought to be, but there were the gossips to think of.

And when the queen of Montcraig chat, Pam McGregor, met them on the way out of the party, Grace knew this would be all over town by tomorrow.

"What's going on here?" the older woman asked, her long hair coming down from its customary tight bun and falling about her face in an untidy mess. Grace suspected she wasn't the only one who'd found her dancing feet tonight.

"Have you been dancing, Pam?" Grace asked from her perch on Sean's back, unable to hide her surprise.

"Aye, I have," Pam replied. "When a gentleman goes to the bother of asking it would be rude to turn him down. Especially at New Year."

"And who's the lucky man?" She shifted on to a more comfortable position on Sean's back. He felt warm and strong and seemed to take her weight easily. The scent of him was deliciously familiar and she had to resist the urge to sigh with contentment.

"Not that it's anything to do with you, but it was Jim Aiken who asked."

Grace was pleased. It seemed he was sticking to his decision to get on with his life at last.

"So, what are you doing on Sean McIver's back?"

As she looked down at Pam's interested expression, Grace decided she no longer cared if she was to be the subject of gossip. Where was the harm in giving the older woman something to talk about?

"It's Sean giving in to his caveman tactics." She laughed as he carried her off, out of the door and down the steps at the front of the hotel. Grace glanced over her shoulder to find Pam McGregor staring after them and she giggled.

It was two-thirty on New Year's Day when Sean carried her up the stairs to her flat.

"Key?" he asked, holding his hand up.

After rummaging in her bag, she handed him her door key. He carried her inside and tipped her on to the sofa.

"That was quite a night."

She laughed, winded by her sudden descent and soft landing.

"Yes, it was. It's years since anyone's given me a piggy back." She sat up to make room for him beside her and dropped her shoe on to the floor. "Really, thank you, Sean. I wasn't looking forward to what the walk would have done to my feet."

His blue eyes crinkled at the corners as he grinned at her. The sofa dipped as he sat beside her.

"Why did you bring the shoe back?"

She shrugged.

"I'm hoping the other one will turn up. They were my favourite pair and they cost a fortune."

"It's bound to be somewhere," he replied reasonably. Then he frowned. "You don't strike me as someone who would spend a fortune on impractical shoes."

"They might be impractical – especially now I've only got one of them. But they're also very lovely."

She saw him frown as he glanced at the discarded shoe.

"It must be a girl thing, because I just can't see it."

"I wouldn't normally," she admitted, "but they called out to me as I passed by them in the shops. Actually, they called to Lizzie, who decided they'd be perfect for me and she made me try them on. And then I was smitten."

He laughed.

"That makes a bit more sense. I can see Lizzie wasting money on shoes."

She smiled as she got to her feet.

"I'll put the kettle on. It's the least I can do, after you've gone to the bother of carrying me all the way back."

He was lying on the sofa when she came back and she suspected that, if she'd been a minute longer, he might have been fast asleep. He brightened up when she handed him his hot drink.

"Thanks."

"That was so sad about Jim and Daisy," she said. She knew a discussion about missed chances was probably not the brightest move on her part, but she couldn't get the tale out of her head.

"Not the way I'd hoped the story would end," he agreed.

"But to find out she'd just carried on – that she'd married and had a family – while all the time he was pining."

Sean leaned forward and put his cup on the coffee table.

"Now he's found out the truth he can get on with his life."

Grace wasn't so sure.

"Can someone really put years of feelings behind them and start again?"

She stopped talking, because somehow the conversation was no longer about Jim and Daisy – it was about her and Sean, and they both knew it. And she didn't want to go there. She didn't want to examine where the future might take them or the effects of their past on their situation today.

"I hope so," Sean said quietly, obviously not sharing her reluctance to examine the situation. "Don't you?"

"We're OK as we are, aren't we, Sean? No need to worry about what happened before. Best just to think about what we have now."

He reached out and took her hand.

"And what about the future, Grace? Do you ever think about our future?"

She didn't know how to answer. If she said yes, he'd want to know her thoughts, and she was scared. He'd left her before. If she allowed herself to think of a future with him and he decided to go travelling without her again, she knew it would devastate her.

"I prefer to think about the present," she insisted. "That's all that's important."

He rubbed his thumb along the back of her hand and she wished he wouldn't, because when he did that she found it hard to think.

"I need to know there's a possibility of a future," he pressed gently. "I don't want to spend years of my life to discover at some point in the distant future that you don't care about me as much as I care about you. I don't want to be another Jim Aiken."

Why did he have to sound so reasonable? Of course he didn't want to be another Jim. Nobody would want that.

"You've only been back five minutes." She tried to keep her tone light. "And we're both still young. You can't expect me to have my life all planned out at the age of twenty-six."

"Of course I don't."

He dropped her hand and she wished he hadn't. But what could she say?

"I'm not ready to make any promises of undying love."

When she saw his expression, she wished she hadn't said anything. The playful grin and the hopeful look in his eye were gone with her refusal to declare her feelings for him.

She had to protect herself. Even though she trusted him now with the present, she couldn't bring herself to place her future in his care. Not just yet.

"It seems there's very little left to say, then."

He got to his feet.

She wanted to stop him leaving. She really did. But how could she, when she couldn't bring herself to give him the assurances he obviously craved?

"Can't we carry on the way we are for now?" she asked desperately.

He looked so sad she wanted to put her arms around him and make his hurt go away. But she sat, immobile and powerless. In all honesty she couldn't tell him she loved him. And she knew that was what he wanted.

"Is that what you want?" he asked. "Companionship with no promises or expectations? Even after seeing what hoping and hanging on can do to someone? After seeing how things didn't work out for Jim and Daisy?"

She nodded. She knew it wasn't what he wanted. But she also hoped he would be willing to do that for her. She hardly dared to breathe as she waited for his decision.

He let out his breath in a whoosh.

"If that's all you're offering – the here and now – then I suppose I don't have much choice."

He didn't look happy about it. She bit her lip.

"I'm sorry, Sean. It's just too soon for me to know what my feelings will be in the future. I enjoy your company. I really like being with you. I can't give you more than that at the moment."

"I'd rather have you in my life on a just-for-now basis, than not have you at all," he told her.

Then he left, without kissing her goodbye.

\* \* \* \*

Sean covered the short distance home quickly. He hated to leave her, but he hated even more that he'd pushed her, yet again, to progress their relationship when she obviously wasn't ready. He was gutted that she'd been unable to give him the answer he wanted.

That was why he'd lost her last time, he reminded himself. Because he'd been too impatient to wait for her. Last time it had been for her agreement to travel; this time it was for a declaration of some sort. For the promise of a future.

One of these days he'd learn. But he did wonder if she would ever give him the words of love that he craved. Was he destined to be another Jim? Madly in love for years with a woman who didn't return his feelings?

# Winter Wedding

GRACE knew she'd upset Sean, but she'd rather know she had answered his question truthfully, than that she'd lied to him.

"Aw, honey." Lizzie draped a comforting arm around her shoulder. "I know it's rough. He's lovely, but you've got to do what's right for you."

They were in the school assembly hall waiting for the members of the drama group to arrive. They would be there any moment, so the girls didn't have long to speak.

Grace knew what Lizzie had said was true. She only wished that what was right for her was what Sean wanted. She nodded in response to Lizzie's advice.

"So where have you left things? Don't tell me you've finished with him?"

"No, but things are strained. He thinks I don't feel as much for him as he does for me. Maybe he's right."

"It's early days," Lizzie told her. "There's no need to rush. When you're ready to think about a future with him, you'll know."

"Is that how it was with you and Ed?"

Lizzie smiled.

"To be honest, I didn't think about Ed in romantic terms at all until very recently."

"But now you know?"

"Yes." Lizzie was adamant and Grace envied her that certainty.

Their window of chatting opportunity slammed shut as Callum walked in with Katie, both laughing and joking.

"Hello, you two!" Grace called out, pleased to see Katie so happy and relaxed. The change in the girl was remarkable. It was amazing what a good friend could do.

And she was sure they were just friends. There wasn't a hint of romance between them. They teased and joked, but were also very supportive of each other. She marvelled at Sean's wisdom in encouraging the friendship. If only that same nature had seen how desperately she had needed him to postpone their year of travelling when they'd left school.

The drama meeting passed quickly. The children were eager to do well. The suggestion they might perform their play on a real stage in a real theatre had ensured they were even more enthusiastic than usual.

"We have to get the theatre ready," Ed said as the children all began to leave. "We can't let them down."

"It will be ready, no problem," Sean assured him. "Everyone's promised to come back to work tonight. The place is almost cleared of all the old junk. All we'll need to do is the cleaning and decorating."

"All?" Grace repeated, thinking of the daunting task ahead. It was true they'd powered through a ton of work. Skips had been filled, papers had been filed and collections of memorabilia had been catalogued. She smiled as she recalled how proud Sean was of that collection and his plans for displaying it once the theatre was in order.

And he was right, it wouldn't take long. Apart from the clear up, they'd even effected most of the repairs that were needed to ensure the building was safe and in good order. All that was left was purely cosmetic.

"I've been meaning to ask," Sean began, "about the old office Grace and I have been clearing." Quickly he explained Grace's idea that he could rent the space as a studio.

Ed nodded.

"That could work for me," he said. "We'll have a little chat about rent and see if we can come to an agreement, then get the committee to formalise the arrangement."

Grace smiled, pleased she'd been the one to think of the idea – and that Sean had listened. It would be beneficial to all. Sean would have somewhere light and bright during the day, and it would provide much-needed regular income for the theatre.

*      *      *      *

They had a good turnout, the best they'd had in months. It seemed that, now the Christmas and New Year celebrations were forgotten, everyone was eager to keep busy during the dark winter nights.

Sean and Grace finished clearing the last of the office that night. It seemed like the end of an era and he couldn't help feeling sad as they walked down the narrow staircase, each with a bin bag in their hands.

He was tempted to reach out for her hand as he'd done on countless other times since that first night, when she'd been nervous about climbing up. It would have been another excuse to touch her. But something stopped him. He guessed she wouldn't appreciate it.

"So, all done." She smiled as they reached the bottom of the stairs and stepped on to the area outside the upper circle. "I wonder where he'll have us working next?"

Sean shrugged a shoulder.

"We'll have to see." He went over to the wide window-sill and picked something up. "But I want you to have this before we join the others."

She took the purple gift bag he held out to her.

"Where did you conjure this up from?"

"I left it here on my way up. Seemed easier than having to bring it up and down those stairs." He knew his explanation made no sense and he didn't know himself why he hadn't handed it over straight away.

But she gave a half smile and peered inside the bag. As he watched, her smile broadened to a grin.

"My shoe! Where did you find it?"

"I went back to the hotel and asked."

"Oh." Her expression slipped. "I phoned and spoke to Reception," she said. "It wasn't in the Lost and Found . . ."

"The cleaner had put it in her cupboard for safe keeping and had forgotten to pass it to Reception. I should have given it to you straight away." He thought for a moment she was angry with him, but then she threw her arms around his neck and kissed his lips. An extreme reaction for finding a shoe, he thought, but he wasn't about to complain.

Ed had them on painting duties next, in opposite sides of the theatre. Sean knew it wasn't on purpose; Ed had merely sent them to where they were needed, but he missed Grace at his side. He hoped it might not do their relationship any harm. Things had been strained since their conversation after he'd carried her home on New Year's morning. A bit of space might do them both good.

*     *     *     *

With very little else to do in Montcraig on the dark and cold winter nights, enthusiasm for the theatre project was running high.

They were ahead of schedule by the time February arrived.

"I think Ed might agree to us taking a break over half term so we can go away for a few days after the wedding," Lizzie confided in Grace as the break approached.

Grace spoke to Sean about that the next day.

"We need to get them a wedding present," she said. "But as they've both been living in their own homes for years, they've already got two of everything!"

Sean nodded.

"Do you want us to pool our resources?"

"Unless you have anything else planned. I was thinking of a couple of nights in a nice hotel?"

"I'll have a look online and see what I can come up

with," he said.

That was the honeymoon and the wedding present sorted in one go. Grace now only needed to persuade Lizzie that she needed to buy a new dress . The other woman had been adamant she didn't need one, but Grace imagined she'd regret it if she married in one of her everyday dresses, as she'd said she was going to do.

"Honestly, Grace, a big flouncy dress isn't me."

Grace had no interest in fashion, but even she knew how much nicer she felt when she made the effort to dress up. And this was going to be an important day.

"Lizzie, this is your wedding we're talking about," she reminded gently. "And this is going to be for ever, isn't it?"

Lizzie flushed.

"Of course it is."

"Then don't you want to mark the occasion out as something special?"

She could see Lizzie thinking. She remained silent, allowing her to reach her own conclusion.

Slowly, Lizzie nodded.

"Yes," she said slowly. "OK, we can go dress shopping. But I don't want anything too fussy."

Grace glanced at Lizzie and smiled reassuringly.

"You'll look stunning, whatever you wear," she told her.

They took a trip into the city that Saturday.

"This is such a waste of time when we could be at home, warm and cosy." Lizzie looked out of the train window. "Looks like that snow might settle."

Grace smiled.

"Travelling in snow is a hazard of living in Montcraig in winter. You've lived there long enough to know that."

Lizzie refused to go anywhere near the wedding shops.

"We could just have a look," Grace tried to persuade her.

Lizzie would have none of it. Instead, she went to a shop she knew, where she bought the floaty dresses and skirts she normally wore.

"They import the clothes," she said to Grace as she searched through the rails. "I know I'll find something unique and something I'll be comfortable in."

She was right, but it wasn't on the rails. When she heard they were looking for a wedding outfit, the owner brought the ideal thing from the back.

"How about this?" she asked, holding up a flowing ivory dress that had been heavily embroidered with gold thread. "It only arrived yesterday, and it has a matching cloak – which I think you're going to need in this weather."

Lizzie tried it on and Grace tried not to cry, failing miserably.

"You look like a bride," she managed at last.

"And, what about you?" Lizzie asked. "I refuse to be the only one looking like a Christmas tree." Her smile softened her words. "If I'm getting dressed up, my maid of honour needs to be suitably dressed, too."

Grace tried on a similar – if slightly less elaborate – dress in red. Something completely unlike anything else in her wardrobe. Even her party dresses were no-nonsense.

As she left the shop, all she could wonder was what Sean would think when he saw her dressed up.

\*     \*     \*     \*

Sean collected Grace on the morning of the wedding. He stood on the doorstep and she saw his jaw drop.

"You look . . . You look . . ."

"Nice?" she finished for him.

He nodded.

"You're not supposed to upstage the bride, you know."

"I won't," she told him with confidence. Lizzie looked like a fairy princess in her dress with its matching cloak. Nothing and nobody could upstage her in that outfit.

It was cold, and Grace was glad for her own cloak as she pulled the folds of material closely about her. Sean went to open the passenger door, but she shook her head.

"We should let Lizzie sit in the front."

They picked Lizzie up next – Ed was making his own way – and they made their way up the windy hillside road to the church.

"It seems odd to be getting married on a Monday," Lizzie said. "But we wanted to be married on the first day of the break and the minister couldn't do later in the day."

"It suits for a celebratory meal," Grace said from the back of the car. "Time for you to get married then we can have lunch at the Montcraig hotel."

"Oh, no. I don't want any fuss," Lizzie said. "I only want to get married and slip quietly away home. I'm moving into Ed's house," she said. "His place is bigger. We're going to rent my place out until we're ready to start a family, then sell both houses so we can buy somewhere bigger."

Lizzie was babbling. Grace found it odd Lizzie was talking about the future. She'd never mentioned having children before. Grace was even more shocked to realise she wanted children some day, too. She'd never given the matter any thought before.

A quick glance at the back of Sean's head made her realise the children she envisaged had his dark hair. And his blue eyes. His smile.

She forced her eyes tightly shut and shook her head in an attempt to block out the images.

\*         \*         \*         \*

Sean didn't want to worry the bride or the maid of honour, but he could feel the wheels of his car slipping on the icy road. The incline was sharp and there were a number of occasions where he'd lost control for a moment.

"Everything OK, Sean?" Grace sounded worried as she called to him from the back of the car.

"All in hand," he replied with more confidence than he felt.

As it turned out, the accident wasn't his fault. He heard Lizzie gasp at his side as a car hurtled down the hillside, completely out of control, its driver hooting and waving for them to get out of the way.

"Sean, do something," Grace cried.

So he took the only option available. He turned the wheel as fast as he could, which had them skidding out of harm's way but meant he lost control completely. His heart pounded and he could hear Lizzie scream as the car spun to face down the hill they'd just driven up, then slid, nose first, into the ditch. The engine stalled.

It was eerily silent. He breathed out then looked around.

"Everyone OK?" Lizzie nodded and he glanced over his shoulder. "Grace?" She was pale with fright and all he wanted to do was gather her close.

"Yes, I'm fine. Are you OK?"

She sounded thoroughly shaken, but he was touched she was worried about him.

"I'm fine," he assured her. "But I've a feeling the car might not be."

He opened the door and an icy blast of winter hillside air rushed in.

Looking a little way down the hill he saw the other driver getting out of her own car. Taking it slowly on the icy road, he walked towards her.

"Pam." He recognised her. "Are you all right?"

As he reached her, he could see she was trembling as she looked first at her own car, then over at Sean's.

"I'm so sorry." She began to sob quietly and Sean put a comforting arm around her shoulder.

"No need to be sorry," he told her. "It was an accident."

"I'd been up at the church to do the flowers and by the time I came out it was snowing again. I've never been able to drive in snow."

"Come and sit in my car." He guided her over and sat her next to Grace. "She's OK," he told the bride and maid of honour. "Just had a bit of a fright."

Grace nodded and reached to give Pam's hand a comforting pat, then glanced quickly at Lizzie.

"We should have been at the church five minutes ago. Is the car OK?"

Sean nodded.

"Seems to be. But we're stuck firmly in the ditch. We're still a bit too far away for you two to walk in those fancy shoes, so we'll need to be pulled out."

"There's no time to call a tow truck." Lizzie bit her lip. "Ed will be wondering where we are. He'll think I'm not going to turn up!"

"He won't think that," Sean said. "But we do need to get to church as soon as we can."

Still trembling, Pam sat forward in her seat.

"Jim might help," she said. "He was on his tractor in the top field when I drove past a moment ago. I'm sure if we ask he'll have us back on the road in a moment."

Sean dug his mobile from his pocket.

"I'll give him a ring."

Jim was there in two minutes. They all got out to allow him to work his magic and, another minute later, the hero of the hour had pulled the car back on to the road.

"Thank you so much." Lizzie threw her arms around him for a quick hug before walking back towards the car.

"I'll pull your car back on to the road, Pam," he said.

But Pam was getting back into Sean's car.

"Not now. I'm going to a wedding!" she insisted.

Jim scratched his head.

"What about the shop? Don't you need to get back?"

Pam shook her head.

"Both the girls are in today."

Sean guessed she was talking about her assistants. He glanced at the bride to see what her reaction was to this gate-crasher!

Lizzie's jaw had dropped, but she recovered quickly and gave a little laugh.

"Why not? You'll be very welcome, too, Jim."

Jim, in his dirty boots and outdoor work clothes, needed no second invitation.

"I'll move the tractor off the road and come with you in the car."

It wasn't long before the wedding party, plus the additional two, were making their way into the church.

The minister met them at the door.

"We were getting worried." He smiled at Lizzie.

She glanced over his shoulder to where Ed was standing at the altar, looking anxiously towards them.

"Sorry. We got held up on the road."

"My boots," Jim said to the minister. "Shall I take them off so I don't bring dirt in?"

"Just come in. We don't have much time. We're running very late and I'm afraid I have somewhere else to be."

Forgetting tradition, Lizzie raced up to Ed's waiting arms. He smiled with relief and their eyes met before he pulled her into a tight embrace.

Sean bit back the aching sense of loss that he would never hold Grace at the altar the same way. Then he quickly looked away. He wasn't being fair to his friends. Just because he wasn't destined to have his happy ever after with the woman he loved, didn't mean he shouldn't be happy for them.

# The Parents Return

ANNIE and Alistair Anderson arrived home on March 1. Grace was excited, but apprehensive, because she needed to tell them about Sean. She couldn't put it off any longer. Her mother looked rested and happy as Grace found her in the kitchen of the family home.

"Darling." Annie Anderson came over and hugged her. "It's wonderful to see you."

"It's lovely to see you, too." Grace kissed her mother's cheek and was cheered as her nose twitched to the familiar scent her mother used. "Tell me all about your holiday."

"Not yet. Not until you've told me about Sean McIver and the reason you kept quiet about the fact he was back."

"Ah." The town grapevine had obviously informed her mother of the news first.

Her mother smiled softly.

"Grace, you know you don't have to hide anything from me. All I want is for you to be happy."

"I know, Mum. And I would have told you, but I didn't want you to worry. Not when you were so far away."

Annie nodded.

"But I worry about you anyway, even when there's nothing wrong. It's my job to worry about you."

"Even though I'm a grown woman?"

"Especially now you're a grown woman. When you were a girl I could keep you close and know you were safe. Now I've had to let you go and have to trust you to look out for yourself."

"Which I'm doing, Mum."

Annie nodded again.

"OK. Your dad's nipped out to get the newspapers, so fill me in quickly before he gets back."

Grace knew her mother wasn't ecstatic. She'd never complained about Sean, but it was obvious from the things Annie didn't say that she was still upset Sean hadn't stuck around all those years.

Grace took a deep breath. There wasn't much to say.

"He suggested we might go travelling together in the summer holidays."

She saw her mother's expression slip.

"Mum, he's changed."

Annie Anderson's face showed she wasn't convinced.

"Darling, people don't change. Not really."

"Well, Sean seems to have. He's a caring teacher and he's becoming involved with the drama group and the project to bring the old theatre back into use."

Annie shook her head.

"It's not like Sean McIver to be so selfless."

Grace winced.

"Mum, that's a bit harsh." It was a sign of how much her mother disliked Sean that she had made the comment. Annie always looked for the best in people. She'd never usually speak about anyone with such negativity.

"I'm sorry, darling, but I'll never forget how he left you devastated when you needed his support."

"He was young."

"So were you. But the trait for that sort of selfishness doesn't disappear. You'd made plans together. It was unforgiveable of him to refuse to wait even a few months for you to go with him."

Grace bit her lip. It was time to confess. She'd allowed her mother to think the worst of Sean because otherwise Annie would have blamed herself for the break-up of Grace's relationship, even though it was nobody's fault. But now Sean was back, it was time to set the record straight.

"Mum, I didn't tell him why I needed to stay."

Annie paled.

"You didn't?"

Grace shook her head.

"You didn't want people knowing, so I kept it to myself. I told him I'd changed my mind. That I wanted to go after university, rather than in our gap year."

She could see the turmoil in her mother's eyes as this piece of information sunk in.

"I know it's a lot to take in, Mum. You're going to have to rethink what you've believed for eight years. But really, it wasn't his fault. He didn't know."

It shocked Grace to realise what she'd said was true. Exactly as her mother had done, she'd blamed Sean for something that wasn't his fault. Even as she'd agreed to friendship and then to going out with him, a part of her had still resented that he'd gone without her.

But it wasn't his fault. It must have seemed to him that she'd been pushing him away, so it was no wonder he'd gone without her. Why hadn't she realised?

"Oh, Grace. If only I'd known. I never would have expected you to give up your future and stay in Montcraig because of me."

"I didn't give up my future, Mum." Grace smiled softly and went over to drape an arm around her mother's shoulders. "And I wouldn't have had it any other way. I wanted to be here while you were getting well."

"But why didn't you say?"

"Because I didn't want you worrying about anyone but yourself. I only told you now because Sean's back and I didn't want you blaming him for something that's my fault."

Her fault. She stifled a gasp. Then, as the door opened and her father came in, his coat dripping with rainwater, she forced herself to put it out of her mind.

"Hi, Dad," she said. "Nice holiday?"

"Hello, Grace." Her dad bent to give her a hug. "We took lots of photos. Do you have time to see them?"

"Of course I have. Why else do you think I came round?"

"To see us?" her mother suggested with a weak smile.

"Ah, yes – that, too."

Grace was still dizzy from the realisation Sean wasn't to blame, but she managed to smile as her father got out his digital camera and proudly displayed the holiday snaps.

She had a quick cup of tea with her parents and then excused herself.

"You'll both need to get settled back in," she told them as she zipped up her anorak and put up her hood. No point taking an umbrella in this weather – their freezing cold winter had morphed into an extremely wet, windy and chilly spring.

As she walked towards home, she thought some more about her confession to her mother. She couldn't quite believe she hadn't realised before. It hadn't been Sean's fault he'd gone. What else could he do, when all she'd told him was that she'd changed her mind?

On impulse, she took a diversion. She needed to sort things out, and she needed to do it as soon as she could.

He came to the door in paint-splattered jeans and shirt.

"I've been working," he told her with a grin. "This will probably be the last painting I finish in this house, though. My studio at the theatre should be ready soon."

She nodded. Then, unable to stop herself, she threw her arms around his neck and held him tight.

He gave a short laugh of surprise, then his hands came up around her waist.

"I'm getting paint on your coat," he told her, his voice muffled against her hair.

"And I'm getting you wet, but I don't care."

"Well, at least come in so I can paint your coat inside where it's dry."

She let him go and followed him into the hall, giving the door a push closed on her way. Then she looked up at him, tears stinging the back of her eyes and her throat.

"I'm sorry," she said.

He stood a short way away in the tiny space and she resisted the instinct that told her to hug him again.

"What for?"

"I'm sorry that I let you think I'd changed my mind about going travelling with you."

He frowned. A dark lock of hair fell on to his forehead and she reached out to brush it back. He gave a hint of a grin as her fingers brushed against his forehead.

"Your hand's cold. And I don't think this is the sort of conversation we should be having in the hallway."

There was a fire roaring in the grate in the living-room. She went up to it and felt its warmth on her face and she held out her hands, wriggling her fingers against the heat.

"So," he said, wiping his hands on his jeans and then taking her coat from her shoulders and draping it over the back of a chair to dry. "What's all this about?"

"I didn't change my mind," she said.

He raised an eyebrow.

"No?"

"No. Well, yes, I suppose I did, but not really. It wasn't because I'd changed my mind about you or about us."

"So why didn't you go with me?"

"It wasn't my decision to make. It's not a secret any longer, so I can tell you, but my mother's been ill."

"I'm sorry."

"She was diagnosed just before we were supposed to leave. She didn't want anyone to know. I've discovered today she hadn't meant to include you in that veil of secrecy."

"I had no idea. I thought you were ending our relationship."

That had never occurred to Grace at the time, but she could see now why he would think that.

"Would it have made a difference? Would you have

stayed if you'd known?"

"How can you ask that? Of course I would have."

"I'm sorry. I just wondered."

Grace's sigh tore at his heart. He couldn't believe he'd left her when she'd needed him. OK, so she hadn't told him about her mother, but he should have known her well enough to realise there had to be a reason she'd changed her mind.

He went over to where she stood at the fireplace and wrapped his arms around her.

"I'm sorry."

She looked up, her big brown eyes confused.

"Why are you sorry?"

"I let you down."

"No." Her voice was fierce. "You didn't."

It seemed they were both intent on taking the blame and that wasn't going to get them anywhere.

"How about we agree it wasn't anyone's fault," he suggested softly and she nodded, her blonde curls bobbing around her shoulders.

"That's a good idea."

He stood for a moment with his arms around her and for the first time in years he felt complete.

Suddenly it made sense. He only wished he'd listened harder all those years ago. She might not have told him outright what the matter was, but she'd given him lots of hints. He could see that now. He'd been so young, so eager to be on his way and so convinced she didn't want to go with him any longer, he hadn't noticed.

"So, we think about the future," he said. "No looking back, no regrets. What's happened is in the past."

"Yes."

He smiled. Finally, he knew coming back to Montcraig had been the right thing to do.

## *Rain, Rain, Rain*

I DON'T remember a time when it wasn't raining." Lizzie was sitting on the window seat in Grace's living-room, looking out as raindrops beat on to the glass.

"That's because this is the wettest spring on record," Grace reminded her.

"And this wind!" Lizzie sighed. "Even if I have a good hair day, within seconds of going out I look a complete mess."

"Do you want to give our shopping trip a miss? We could have a girly afternoon in with ice-cream and a DVD. I've got that new one about the group of women who were at uni together, then meet up twenty years later?"

"I do want to see that film." Lizzie took another glance at the rain and frowned. "I'm tempted. But I need to get a birthday present for Ed. His birthday is on Wednesday, so if I don't get him something this weekend he'll be stuck with the only things I can buy in Montcraig – socks and a bar of chocolate."

Grace smiled.

"He won't mind." And she knew that was true, because it was common knowledge that, as far as Ed was concerned, all his birthdays and Christmases had arrived the day he'd married Lizzie!

"I know. But I should get him something special. This is the first occasion we've celebrated as a married couple."

Grace nodded.

"I need to get something for Mum, too. Hers is tomorrow. Come on, let's get it over with and then maybe we'll have time to watch that DVD when we get back."

Grace drove them into the neighbouring town. The few shops in Montcraig didn't offer enough choice if you were looking for a special gift. Besides, it was nice to have a change of scenery. The dark winter days had made travelling any distance an unpleasant experience and, now it was supposedly spring, it was important they made the effort to get out and about.

She found something for her mother pretty quickly – a lovely bracelet she knew Annie would like. Ed was a little harder to buy for, though – at least from Lizzie's point of view. Grace took the easy option and bought him a box of chocolates that she happened to know were his favourites. She could get away with that, as she wasn't his new wife.

They scoured the shops with no luck.

"Why don't we go for a coffee?" Lizzie suggested.

They'd barely sat down with their lattes when they noticed three of their teen pupils – Callum, Katie and Sadie – at a nearby table.

"Hello, Miss Anderson. Hello, Mrs Price," they chorused. Katie and Sadie smiled at them both and Callum gave a cheeky grin.

"Not out with your boyfriend today, Miss Anderson?"

She raised an eyebrow and the teenager laughed.

"I know, he's not your boyfriend."

As they watched the teenagers leave, Lizzie leaned forward across the table.

"You're still telling people he's not your boyfriend?"

"Of course not. But I don't think it's a good idea to encourage the pupils to gossip about our private lives."

Lizzie sat back with a sigh.

"I suppose you're right."

Grace was silent for a moment as she thought about her situation. When Sean had come back she'd been horrified at the thought of gossip. Now, though, it didn't seem like the worse thing in the world. Depending, of course, on what they were saying.

"About the gossip," she began and Lizzie looked back at

her, feigning innocent. "How bad is it?"

Lizzie laughed.

"Not bad. You know Montcraig – not a lot goes on, so everyone makes the most of anything that happens. Mine and Ed's wedding took some of the heat off you two, of course."

Grace laughed.

"You say that as if you went and got married as a favour to me!"

"Maybe we did." Lizzie's eyes were smiling over the top of her coffee cup.

"In that case I'm very grateful. You went above and beyond the call of friendship!" They both giggled, then Grace's smile faded. "I hope the new theatre will give them something useful to discuss."

"It might," Lizzie said. "But I doubt it."

Somehow Grace doubted it, too.

"You know I don't gossip," Lizzie said to Grace. "So why don't you tell me what's going on with you and Sean? One minute you're insisting you're nothing more than friends, and the next you're barely out of each other's company."

Grace knew it was only fair that she confided in Lizzie. They'd been friends a long time, and she knew she could trust her.

"The thing is, I think I love him."

Beyond a slight widening of her eyes, Lizzie didn't betray any sign of surprise.

"I see." She stirred her coffee, even though she'd already done so. "Have you told him?"

"Not yet."

"Are you going to tell him?"

Grace looked at her friend in horror. She hadn't thought that far. Yes, she'd apologised and, yes, she'd rightfully accepted the blame for what had happened before, but admitting she loved him – well, how was she supposed to do that?

"I don't know how he'll take it."

Lizzie looked surprised.

"Don't you?"

"It's not something you can just drop into the conversation without warning."

"Well, if you want my advice, he hasn't been hanging around for no reason. I suspect he loves you, too. Very much."

Maybe he did. But telling him how she felt was still a very big step.

"We'd better go and see about this present for your husband," Grace said, eager to change the subject. She couldn't help but think that, even though Lizzie was her closest friend, she'd maybe said too much.

"I think a book of poetry," Lizzie said as they made their way back on to the street. "It's something he can keep and I can write a meaningful message inside."

"Good idea. But which book."

Lizzie led the way to the bookshop.

"I think I know the exact one."

\*          \*          \*          \*

Ed had decided against a party for his birthday. All he wanted was a meal at home with his wife, which sounded like a very sensible idea to Grace.

Her mother, also, had decided against a large celebration.

"I really don't need the fuss, darling," she'd replied when Grace had made the suggestion. "Just a quiet birthday tea, with maybe a cake, will be fine."

Of course, Grace took Sean with her. It seemed the natural thing to do. And now she'd cleared up the misunderstanding over him leaving, she knew Annie would be happy to see him.

"Come in," her father greeted them.

As they stepped over the threshold, her dad took their coats.

"These don't seem too wet, considering."

"We drove, Dad."

"But it's only a five-minute walk."

"Five-minute swim, more like!" She giggled.

Her dad nodded in agreement.

"I suppose so." He offered Grace a warm hug and Sean a hearty handshake, then led them into the living-room, where her mother was sitting on the sofa.

Annie was equally welcoming, substituting the handshake her husband had offered Sean for a peck on the cheek.

"What about this rain?" her mother commented. "We certainly didn't bring the weather back with us, did we, Alistair?"

"No, it was glorious for the whole six months we were away," he confirmed.

"Grace told me about your cruise," Sean said as he accepted a slice of cake from Annie. "Did you enjoy it?"

"Oh, yes," Annie said. "It was wonderful. You should try it some time."

Grace held her breath. She knew her mother was only making conversation and wasn't trying to prove a point, but the comment was a bit too close to the reason for her and Sean's separation for comfort.

Sean smiled, his glance clashing with Grace's.

"I've no plans in that direction at the moment," he said.

"You have no plans to travel again?" Annie made the question sound casual, but Grace still couldn't breathe.

"Maybe a summer holiday, but no more than that." He maintained eye contact with Grace. "There's plenty to keep me busy in Montcraig at the moment."

Grace smiled back, relieved to hear his answer. Maybe Lizzie was right. Maybe it was time to trust him and tell him exactly how much he meant to her.

And now she'd decided, she wanted to tell him as soon as she could.

They didn't stay long. They were expected at the theatre by early evening along with all the other volunteers and they were eager to be there. The end was in sight now and everyone was keen to see the finished project.

But all Grace could think of as she drove them the short distance towards home was her need to confess her feelings to him.

"Do you want to come back to my place for a cup of tea before we need to head off to the theatre?" she asked.

"I drank enough tea at your parents' house to last me a while."

She felt the bitter sting of disappointment. She'd wanted to talk to him.

"Still, it would be nice to spend some time alone with you before we have to go off and join the others."

Immediately her heart soared.

"You make the theatre sound like a chore." She parked the car and they both sprinted to the door.

"Well, it is hard work," he said as they climbed the stairs to her flat. "You have to admit that, however worthy and useful to the community the project is."

"We're nearly done," she reminded him. "A couple more evenings should see it all finished. Then we won't know what to do with our time. Although you'll be able to start using your new studio."

They went into her living-room and he turned and caught her hand before they'd even taken their coats off.

"You'll have to come with me. I can paint your portrait."

She felt herself blush.

"You don't want to do that. I'm sure there are other subjects much more worthy of your attention."

Her gaze fixed on his thumb as he stroked the pulse point

at her wrist, driving her out of her mind in the process.

"I can't think of anyone I'd rather paint."

She looked up into his very handsome face and felt her heart flutter.

"Really?"

"Really." His gaze fixed on her lips and she sighed softly as his head descended towards hers. When their lips met, she knew Lizzie was right – she really did have to tell him how she felt.

He pulled away a fraction and she stood in the circle of his arms. A feeling of belonging washed over her and she knew at that point that she did see a future with him. A future with the children she wanted – the ones with the same dark hair and laughing blue eyes as Sean's.

She knew then she wanted to be for ever with Sean.

"Do you remember . . .?" She stopped and cleared her throat. He was smiling softly down at her and she averted her eyes and busied herself with picking imaginary fluff off his jacket. "You know on Christmas Day, you were asking what kind of wedding I'd want?"

"What?" He stopped and took a breath. She was looking up at him with huge brown eyes and he thought he knew where she was going with this conversation. But if he'd got it wrong he could make things between them worse. And if he was wrong he didn't think he would be able to bear it. "What are you trying to say, Grace?"

"I'm ready to think about my future. Our future."

These were the words he'd waited to hear her say and he wanted to pick her up and dance around the room. But they'd been so close to this before and she'd always retreated. He needed to be certain that this time she wouldn't change her mind.

"Are you sure?"

She nodded.

He brought his lips down to hers to seal the promise.

# A Hospital Dash

THEY stood inside the hallway of Grace's flat and looked out at the rain. Giant drops bounced off the street and left water lying inches deep on the tarmac.

"We'll have a poor turn out tonight," she guessed. "I don't think people will want to go out in this."

"Which makes it more important that we make the effort." She looked up at the sky.

"Do you think we should drive?"

"It's even closer than your parents' house. People will laugh if we turn up in the car. Come on, let's make a run for it." He took her hand and pulled her out into the rain and she laughed as the shock of the cold water was blown under the hood of her waterproof anorak and into her collar.

"Wind's picked up again," she called to him as they ran, hand in hand, the short distance to the theatre.

She was right about the poor turnout.

"Only the four of us again." Ed frowned.

"We'll manage," Lizzie said. "There's not much left to do." He nodded.

"We have made good progress."

"We've made fantastic progress," Grace told him. "We're so lucky to have this lovely theatre. Montcraig is very lucky that you convinced everyone to get involved."

Ed smiled.

"We got a booking today."

"That's fantastic!" the other three cried.

"How did you manage that?" Sean asked. "I didn't think you'd done any publicity."

"The father of one of the pupils in the drama group," he shared. "He's in a band and they have a lot of local support. They've booked a night the week after the drama group will stage their play here."

It was looking good and Grace couldn't have been happier for her friend. Ed had worked so hard and he wanted this so much for the community. He deserved the theatre to be a respected venue.

It seemed unbelievable, though, that after all these months of work, it was all practically done.

"We should have a party," Grace suggested. "To celebrate. Let everyone see what a fantastic venue we have here."

"That's a good idea," Ed said. "We'll get something organised. Maybe after the drama group performs the play. We could even have dancing in the stalls." The seats were removable for that reason – and for the pop and rock acts they hoped they might attract in future. The audience for those kinds of shows would want to be on their feet.

"We just thought we could have a general tidy-up tonight," Lizzie said. "And have a general look around and make a list of any outstanding jobs we need to see to."

"Grace and I'll start at the top." Sean grinned. "We've a soft spot for that admin office."

"Your new studio," Lizzie amended. "And a very romantic place, by all accounts."

Grace and Sean laughed along with Lizzie's good-natured teasing, but the smiles were quickly replaced by frowns as they entered the new studio.

"Oh, no! Look at that." Grace looked on, horrified, as water dripped through the ceiling in a couple of places.

"We've probably lost a couple of tiles off the roof in that wind. But I'm going to go up into the roof space to make sure it's not a leaking water pipe."

He dug his torch out from the pocket of his jacket and climbed up, while Grace went in search of Ed and Lizzie. They needed to know what was happening and that there might be a potential problem.

"I checked the roof from the street," Ed admitted. "And

I couldn't see any evidence we'd lost any roof tiles on the ground around the building. But I suppose a couple might have been dislodged with all the wind we've had recently."

He took the stairs to the upper office two at a time and was at the top before Grace had even put a foot on the first step. Just as she did step on the stair, there was an almighty crash from the office.

She froze, staring at Ed who was equally immobile. Then, heart racing, she ran up the narrow staircase on which she'd never felt safe.

There was a huge mess in the office and she could see an arm poking out of the debris. Sean was under a pile of plaster and wood that littered the floor.

"Sean!" Grace realised with a start that the scream had come from her as she rushed over and started to dig through the debris.

"He must have fallen through the ceiling," Ed said. "I'll phone for an ambulance."

On some level, Grace was aware Lizzie had joined them. She and Ed were soon helping to move the fragments of ceiling off Sean.

Finally, there he was, stone still and deathly pale. Grace wasn't even sure he was breathing.

Nausea threatened to overwhelm her.

Lizzie kneeled at his side and put fingers on his wrist.

"There's a strong pulse," she said.

Grace collapsed to her knees, relief making her legs weak. Ed put a comforting hand on her shoulder.

"The paramedics are on their way. I'm going to wait for them in the foyer, but Lizzie will keep you company."

As Grace waited, feeling helpless, she made a mental note to go on a first aid course at the first available opportunity, because it was ridiculous that the only one of the four present who could have helped was the person out cold.

Help arrived quickly, though, and it seemed no time at all

before Sean was being carried, still unconscious, down to the waiting ambulance.

"Can I come along?" Grace asked as she jogged behind the stretcher. "I'm his girlfriend."

"Of course, love," one of the paramedics confirmed.

She was told to sit in the waiting-room while Sean's injuries were assessed. Ed and Lizzie arrived shortly afterwards and she stepped into Lizzie's comforting hug, tears falling down her face.

"What if he dies?" she asked.

Lizzie forced a laugh.

"Of course he won't die."

But Grace noticed the worried glance she sent in Ed's direction and that made her even more frightened.

It seemed a lifetime before a nurse approached them, although in reality it was probably less than half an hour.

"How is he?" Grace asked.

The nurse smiled and Grace took that as a good sign.

"He's going to be fine. We're going to keep him in for observation because he lost consciousness, but there are no bones broken. He's woken up now and he's asking for you."

Even lying in his hospital bed, bruised and groggy from pain medication, Sean was still so gorgeous it wasn't true. He grinned when he saw her, and then groaned as even that tiny movement caused pain.

Grace smiled softly as she went to sit by his bedside. Her hand hovered over his and she winced as she saw the bruises on it.

"I want to hold your hand, but I'm scared to touch you."

He wiggled his fingers.

"They're fine," he told her.

Her heart ached to see him being so brave when he was obviously in a great deal of pain. She reached out and touched her fingertips to his, still not daring to hold his hand in case she hurt him.

He closed his eyes for a moment and she thought the medication might have made him go to sleep. But then his eyes opened, bright blue and fixed straight on her with such intensity her breath caught.

"You know I love you, right? I want you to know."

She nodded.

"Yes, I do know, Sean. And I love you, too."

As she watched his lips twitched into something resembling a smile.

"I've waited a long time to hear you say that again."

She smiled. She'd waited a long time to feel able to tell him, but now was not the time to confess that. She reached her fingers out to stroke his.

"Do you remember what happened?"

His breath hissed out.

"I don't know." He shook his head and winced. "One minute I was waving the torch around, looking to see where the roof was leaking, the next I was crashing through the ceiling. I don't remember anything until I woke up here."

"I don't think I've ever been so frightened." She sighed. "I should be cross that you put yourself in danger like that."

"I didn't put myself in danger. I'm not a hero, Grace. It was an accident."

She nodded.

"Maybe. But you should have waited until daylight to try to find out where the water was coming from."

"I had my torch," he reminded her. "There was water dripping through. There are probably a couple of roof tiles missing after the recent winds."

"That still doesn't explain how you fell through the ceiling," she commented softly.

He laughed then winced.

"I was so busy looking at the roof, I missed my footing and came off the joist. The lath and plaster wouldn't hold my weight."

She shivered and gripped his hand tightly.

"And now you're badly hurt!"

"Worth it." He grinned. "To have you admitting you love me!"

She laughed softly and then leaned forward – being careful not to hurt him – and pressed her lips against his.

\*              \*              \*              \*

The holes in the roof and the ceiling were mended way before Sean's injuries healed, but Grace was grateful he was back to normal for the official opening of the theatre.

They sat together in the front row and watched as the drama group kicked off proceedings with a performance of Ed's play. It received a standing ovation.

Grace and Sean stood up along with the others and clapped as loudly as they could.

"I can't believe Lizzie and Ed managed to produce something so polished!" Grace whispered in Sean's ear as they applauded. "They were nowhere near ready last week."

The applause faded as Ed, on stage, held up his hand.

"Thank you for attending this evening. This means a lot to the drama group and the theatre's investors, committee and volunteers." He turned to face the pupils lined up for the applause. "Well done, all of you. You were all fantastic." The crowd applauded again and somebody whistled. It was a couple of minutes before Ed was able to continue his speech. "We're hoping this place will bring business into the town and provide a focus for our community."

There was a general murmur of approval.

"I'm not going to stay here chatting all night," Ed continued. "We have a celebration buffet ready in the bar area. I hope you'll all join us."

The audience was in a mood to show appreciation and there was another round of applause before everyone began to file out in search of food and drink to complete the celebrations.

Annie and Alistair Anderson battled against the crowd and came to speak to Grace and Sean.

"The children were very good." Annie smiled. "The theatre looks great – even better than it did when I was a girl."

Grace nodded.

"A lot of people have worked hard to bring this together."

She turned to watch her parents walking off in the same direction as everyone else and saw Pam and Jim following on, chatting and laughing together.

"Do you think there's anything going on?" Sean asked as he and Grace waved across the stalls to the older couple.

"They've been getting on so well these past few months, I hope there's romance in the air," she replied with a smile. Now she and Sean were settled, she wanted the same happiness for everyone else, too.

Sean smiled.

"It would be nice if they got together officially."

Pam and Jim had both allowed early disappointments to keep them from moving forward. As she watched them make their way towards the buffet, Grace hoped they'd now be able to look to the future, just as she and Sean were.

They had the stalls to themselves now and Sean wound his arms around her waist and drew her closer.

"Careful," she warned. "I don't want you to get hurt."

He laughed.

"Thank you for worrying, but the cuts and bruises have healed nicely. Besides, I've wanted to do this all evening," he said as his head descended.

As Grace raised her lips to meet him, they heard giggling and drew apart – although Sean still held his arms tightly around her.

She smiled when she spotted Katie and Callum.

"Your scenery looked fab," she told them. "Well done."

Katie blushed and Callum grinned.

"Thanks, miss," they chorused.

"Yes, well done," Sean echoed.

Callum grinned some more than looked at Grace.

"Miss Anderson, can I ask you a question, please?"

"What is it, Callum?"

"Well, you keep telling me Mr McIver's not your boyfriend," Callum teased, to Katie's obvious amusement. "So why are your arms around him? And why did it looked as though you were about to kiss him?"

In the circle of Sean's arms, she sighed.

"Mr McIver's most definitely not my boyfriend." She looked up into Sean's eyes and smiled. Then she broke the habit of her teaching lifetime as she discussed her personal life with her pupils. "He is, in fact, my fiancé."

The End.

© Suzanne Ross Jones, 2013.

Published in Great Britain by D. C. Thomson & Co., Ltd.,

Dundee, Glasgow and London.

Don't miss our next Pocket Novel No. 730, THE LETTER,
a captivating mystery by Val Bonsall.

On sale May 9, 2013.

If you are looking for back numbers please telephone 0800 318846
Printed and bound by CPI Group (UK) Ltd., Croydon, CR0 4YY